I0731549

If Love Were Salt

A Novel

Also by Sara Salam

If Water Were Fire, A Novel

The Mind Is Just Like A Muscle: A Self-Help Book for Teens
on Growing Up In Modern America

My Truth Journal

Love Isn't Linear: A Collection of Poems About
Modern Love

My Newport: A Collection of Poems About
Newport Beach, California

Remember When: A Collection of Poems by a Lovestruck
Teen Who Had the Courage to Dream

If Love Were Salt

A Novel

Sara Salam

The Peacock Pen Press

2020

ISBN: 978-1-953636-03-4 (Paperback)
ISBN: 978-1-953636-04-1 (Hardcover)
ISBN: 978-1-953636-05-8 (eBook)

Library of Congress Control Number: 2020916850

1. Coming of Age
2. Friendship
3. Family Dynamics
4. Multiculturalism
5. #Ownvoices
6. Diversity
7. Bullying
8. Teen- Young Adult
9. Wellness
10. Mental Health

This is a work of fiction. Names, characters, places, and incidents are either the product of the author's imagination or are used fictitiously, and any resemblance to actual persons, living or dead, businesses, companies, events, or locales is entirely coincidental.

Book cover design by Aspen Denita.
Author portrait by Christina Wehbe.
Edited by Anna Alger.

Icons from the Noun Project:
Ocean by Olena Panasovska.
Anchor by Mungang Kim.

Page 41: *The Young Woman, Old Woman Ambiguous Figure*, or *My Wife and My Mother in Law*, was created by an unknown artist and later re-produced by William Ely Hill. Originally published in Puck Magazine, 1915. Public Domain.

Printed by The Peacock Pen Press in the United States of America.

First Printing Edition 2020.

🌐 www.bysarasalam.com

📷 @bysarasalam

▶ Sara Salam

For those who love.

Prologue

Ryan

Today was supposed to be a good day. We were graduating high school and moving on to college. The end of a chapter, the beginning of another—blah, blah, blah. But it was one of those days where the morning leaves you hopeful with the promise of a sunny day, but the afternoon ends up being a huge disappointment.

On so many levels. The weather, for one. June gloom crept in like an uninvited party crasher. But also, all my emotions. I love Sammy; I do. But I've debated, time and time again, whether it's time to part ways. The dominant male consensus from my people— my friends, my family—is that it's a good thing to be single, a maverick. But for the life of me, I can't understand what's so good about being lonely. Hormones and hearts often cross paths, but I know I could never be happy with one night stands. Which seems like what I would be choosing, if I chose to break up with Sammy.

We haven't talked about breaking up much, not really. But it's been on my mind for a while. A lot. Here I am, fearing the end, and she has no idea. Do we really have to end just because I'm going to college? Is there someone else out there who is better for me?

A few years ago, I lost my virginity to an older woman. She was maybe four or five years older than me. She was fun and everything. We saw each other a lot. I realized that human sexuality isn't so much emotion as it is pure thirst. We hunger for the touch, the temptation of another, and relish the pleasure. But after this girl (woman?) and I hooked up, I'd feel empty. As a man, I don't feel like I'm allowed to feel that. But I do. What was missing with her was love. My heart craved someone to be close to; it needed someone to laugh and cry with. Lusting after something so temporary did not satiate that more important need. I finally found it with Sammy.

The ironic thing is, we (the collective "we," i.e., humans) spend so much time wanting a feeling that is so temporary.

Adding another layer, we (Sammy and I) have our own issues when it comes to sex. Meaning, she won't have it with me. I get it— she's "young." But when does too young become old enough?

Sammy has always had a subtle way of looking at me and saying with her eyes, "It's all right, we will never be far from each other's hearts."

When we embrace, I feel everyone around us, and I cling to her as if I'm afraid she will be swept away by the wind. I savor the feeling of having her so close to me. My heart would like to think that she and I will be together forever. As long as I believe that, my love for her could never end. However, that nagging feeling lingers.

She doesn't know I was crying for the better part of the morning. And I'm not going to tell her. I don't want to burden her with those emotions. I cry a lot anyway. My mom doesn't like it. Neither does my dad. I think they think it's Sammy's fault, that I cry so much. But really, it's because I'm a sensitive soul. I couldn't tell them that, though. I don't think they'd understand. I'd rather they think it's

Sammy's fault. That's a terrible thing to say, to do, but I'm protecting myself. What's the expression—"You have to save yourself before you can save others"? I think this is a solid application of that adage.

I sound more secretive than I'm trying to be. My intentions are pure. We live in a world where we're bombarded with ideas and emotions, through all kinds of methods and mediums. It's overwhelming, not only to live in it, but to think about what the future will bring, the madness. Humans ourselves do not have a complete understanding of who we are, what we wish to gain from life. To learn about ourselves, we ask others. We ask our friends and families what they think of us, how they see us, what we should do. In this regard, we are an incomplete species. How can we understand ourselves better?

I know one thing: I love this girl, this young woman, this person who has opened me up in ways I never thought possible. She's my relief, my joy, my motivation for wanting everything I want out of life. She has this fire that complements this coolness about her. She gives me perspective I can't find anywhere else—a point of view not many share, but probably should. She's wise beyond her years in that way. An old soul, like me. A romantic, like me. A girl who bestowed faith in my heart.

Faith is important to me. And she has faith in me. Even if it isn't the religious kind. Sammy says religion is a narrative for belief, for morals, a story to give power to ideas. She's right.

I love this girl, for all that she is and all that she helps me to be. But is that enough?

I graduated today. This should be a happy day. And I *am* happy. But I'm also blissfully bombarded with feelings. I should share them with Sammy. I will. I should. I plan to. We've got our whole lives ahead of us.

But first, summer.

Chapter 1

"*I* have dreams about you naked."

His words, not mine.

First of all, I'm not that honest, especially with boys.

Secondly, well . . . I'm in too much shock from the direct and sexiful nature of this statement to even contemplate a "secondly."

Am I toeing some kind of boundary here? Talk about your "Blurred Lines."

Also, why am I the one feeling like the guilty party? I haven't done anything wrong.

I don't think. Yet.

I guess I'm not totally sure what is considered "acceptable" when it comes to conversations with someone who may or not be overtly flirting with you, who is teasing you about your panty line, who is *not* your boyfriend.

Let me back up a bit.

I've been with Ryan, my beau, for the better part of the last year. We've had our highs, our lows, our ebbs and flows. We met officially in drama class last year, but he saw me first while he was working at Tower 11 at the beach on Labor Day. So he says. He's a lifeguard. I feel like he saw me before that. I'm still teasing that admission out of him.

Our meet-cute was rather cute. Our first date was at the Fun Zone, which was actually really fun. We've gone to movies, book stores, leisurely strolls, and Prom. I watch him surf at Blackies, 56th, and other spots around town. He comes to yoga class with me. We eat Sidecar Donuts together. We still write poems to each other, though admittedly they are fewer and further between. Probably because the *honeymood* phase is over and we're running out of ways to compliment each other.

Though, love—including ours—isn't linear and ever-climbing. It's twisty, convex, even a little concave (math humor). We serpentine as the best, most devoted couples do. The key is finding your way back (forward?), preferably together but sometimes apart.

A few months ago, Ryan graduated from high school and started classes at OCC in August. I, on the other hand, remain tethered to the horrors of high school as a sophomore. It's different, being in a relationship that seriously could be considered long distance, in comparison to the rigamaroles of typical teen romance. I miss him carrying my books to class and leaving cutesy notes in my locker. Because that's what true love is made of. But we're faring all right.

After Prom, graduation, and a sunny summer, we've entered a new normal.

Which apparently consists of me tempting Taurus.

You see, it started after school one day, when I went with Mama to pick up my brother Andrew from basketball practice. We were sitting in the car in the parking lot of the YMCA off of University Drive. The kids practice in the gym adjacent to the weight room, which is not accessible to the main entrance where we waited.

Andrew, true to form, was the last kid to walk out of practice. He was *always* the last kid to leave anything—the classroom, a birthday party, the beach. I think it's a testament to his easygoing nature, rather than an inherent lack of urgency. Actually, maybe it is inherent. After all, our personalities are rooted in biology. I personally fall on the opposite side of the spectrum from my brother in this regard. For whatever reason, I feel compelled to always be moving—preferably forward—toward something, and at an-opposite-of-glacial pace. That goes for the tangible and intangible. I'm not great at resting.

I digress.

"Hey bro, how was practice?" I greet him as I turn over my right shoulder from the passenger seat while he opens the back door of our Lexus SUV.

Clad in his oversized Kobe "8" jersey and UCLA basketball shorts, he settles into the middle back seat before responding with a monosyllabic, "Good."

It's funny how we always fight over the middle seat. When does *anyone* ever fight over a middle seat? Not on an airplane . . . not on the bus . . . not in a kayak . . . Now that I think about it, it's kinda strange.

We do use what's supposed to be the arm rest as some kind of alternative booster seat so our view of the road is better. So there's that. Probably not super safe.

As I turn back around and Mama begins her thoughtful interrogation of the new plays Andrew learned, how many points he scored, whether he's starting the next game, I notice a svelte six-foot semblance of a person approaching the car.

Who. Is. That?

He's homely-looking, but in a KJ Apa kind of way. Not really my type, but he carries himself with this confidence that is comparable to that of a wolf; not overly imposing, but regal in his gentle strength. He is a coach, after all. So that is helpful. (I may be extrapolating, but who cares—he's easy on the eyes.)

His gait quickens as he approaches our car.

Yikes, he's approaching our car. Why is he doing that? I didn't plan for this.

Granted, I also didn't plan to date Ryan, so there's that.

Ah, yes, Ryan.

I've adopted a "look, don't touch" approach when it comes to appreciating attractive boys from afar. The boundary of what "afar" entails is still defining its borders. There's an ongoing war, and the signing of a treaty is days, maybe weeks from reality.

Did I just liken my relationship to the consequences of war?

Defectors, these hazel cones of light.

"Hey dude, you forgot your water bottle." The first words I ever hear him speak, forever etched in my brain. He taps on Andrew's window and lightly tosses the black Hydro Flask through the opening. Mama rolls down my window before I realize it.

When I do, I forget to breathe.

"Thank you, Dustin, I'm surprised he hasn't lost it yet." Mama beams toward the limby boy as he shifts his attention to her, and after, to me.

"No worries, Mrs. Selim, Andrew really brought it today. We'll be ready for our game on Thursday." He smiles—genuinely, I think—at Mama before he reaches his hand through the window and offers me an invitation into the exchange.

"I don't think we've met," he acknowledges. "I'm Dustin, Andrew's coach."

He's a charmer, this one. I'm in trouble.

"I'm Sam, Andrew's sister and resident cheerleader."

He stifles a laugh and flashes a toothy grin accompanied by dimples that should be illegal. They contour his face like wind-seared sand dunes.

From what I noticed.

"Nice to meet you, Sam. See you at Thursday's game?"

"You can find me in the bleachers with the other cheerleaders. A.K.A., my mom."

I shoot her a knowing look, and she just laughs her hearty midwestern laugh. She gets me.

"See you then," He signs off as he double-taps the side of the door and walks away.

Phew, *that* was unexpected—and, quite frankly, a little exciting.

Andrew didn't notice. He's ten; he doesn't pick up on these vibes just yet. But he will be a heartbreaker when he's older. Mark my words.

Mama, on the other hand, just drives. I know what she's thinking.

At the game that Thursday, Dustin finds us in the stands and moseys over to say hello, *before* tip-off. How do you like that? I guess gameface isn't so relevant when you're coaching a YMCA team, where the stakes are nil compared to, say, high school, where winning is everything, plus a scholarship plus bragging rights plus a girlfriend on the dance team.

I'm sitting with Mama. Daddy didn't come to this one. He's in a trade and goes to bed early. It's already 7 p.m.

How fortuitous.

Dustin skirts along the baseline with the bleachers on his right. I pretend I don't see him and casually turn my head towards the opposite end of the gym, as if to be captivated by the manual scoreboard that looks like something akin to Fenway Park's Green Monster, only chalkboard black.

I think I sold it.

His pupils dig into my profile as he navigates the sea of parents and other family members towards our row, four benches back.

How do I know this, if I'm so consciously avoiding eye contact?

It's a gift.

He approaches to my left and hovers unwittingly next to a toddler teething on a binky shaped like a butterfly. I feel my heart flutter. The irony is not lost on me.

He says hi to Mama first, per modern wooing etiquette. On seeing his choice of greeting—a gentle handshake—I approve.

Then, as he moves his gaze towards mine, I see it—the flicker of ferocity, the look that gives it all away. It only lasts for a flash, just enough time for someone who is (honestly) looking for it, like Carmen San Diego.

"Hi Sam," he all but whispers, "it's nice to see you again. I hope you enjoy the game."

Which is probably code for: *It's nice to see you and I hope we can enjoy each other someday soon.*

As coyly as possible, I smile what I think is a flirtatious yet noncommittal grin, and say, "Hello Dustin, good luck tonight."

That's how flirting works, right?

With Ryan, I didn't really even realize I was doing it. Flirting. It just kinda happened. I felt more at ease, more natural. Like I knew exactly what I wanted to say and how I wanted to say it, before I could consciously string together the words—like that perfect song lyric that so accurately describes a feeling like nothing else you ever heard before.

Flirting on purpose is so much harder than flirting on accident.

Honestly, I couldn't even tell you how the game went, as my interest was so unabashedly zoned in (pun intended) between the players' bench and baseline of the basketball court.

I do know they won. Yay team.

After the game, I'm minding my own business, loitering outside the entrance to the gym, checking my Instagram to see what eventful happenings had taken place up until that moment in the world of Balboa Bay High School and beyond.

Some cursory glances allow me to observe Dustin yucking it up with some of who I assume are his friends from school, coaches on the opposing team.

He must be so excited he can maintain bragging rights in light of the game's outcome.

I see him see me, our eyes catching each other like falling stars— only noticed when you're meant to notice them, so often missed it's like they never happened in the first place.

He departs his clique with a token nod and bro hug—the one where each person locks their right hand in each other's and half-hugs their counterpart with the other—before moseying, no, *strutting*, in my direction.

I'm alone and shaking subtly.

"Fraternizing with the enemy?" I coax as he approaches me, in an attempt to hide my nervousness.

"That was reconnaissance," he counters effortlessly. "Even though we won, you can never be too prepared for next time."

"Ah," I acknowledge. "A planner, how refreshing."

"Not so much a planner as a man who hates to lose."

"Fair enough."

Silence.

I glance towards the ground as I shift my weight between my feet, which are strapped in Kork-Ease low-platform wedges. Eye contact could be fiery.

"Do you go to BBHS?" he asks, innocently enough. "I know Andrew goes to Eastcliff, even though he plays in this league."

"I do," I confirm. "We transferred a few years ago. We live on the peninsula."

"That's right, Andrew mentioned that. Fun place to grow up."

"I like it. I'm sure I'll appreciate it more as an adult."

He stifles a laugh.

"Just being honest." Did I overshare?

"For a sixteen-year-old, you're pretty mature."

"Fifteen," I correct him. "And yes, I've always been mature for my age. Sometimes I wonder when my age will catch up with my soul."

"Judging from that statement, it probably won't be until you're thirty."

"So you're judging me now?" I sneer, playfully of course.

"Only in the best sense of the word," he replies, this time with a wink.

Reminds me of Ryan's winks. My stomach turns.

"So, Sam," he continues, "maybe we could talk again sometime, like on the phone, or on FaceTime."

"So you can judge me some more?"

"Yeah, and so I can tell you what I really think about you."

Oh crap, I'm in trouble.

"Can't wait," I manage to squeak.

He takes my phone and saves his contact info as "Dustin Peterson, Magic Maker."

Ooooooookay.

And so, here we are.

Dustin is, well, a great many things—including an academic all-star and team captain of Newport Cove's wrestling team.

Not only is he coaching my little brother's U-12 basketball team, he's insanely intelligent and fun to talk to.

Plus he makes me feel a little . . . dangerous.

At fifteen, my hormones knowingly betray my feelings in favor of sometimes raunchy, on-the-verge-of-R-rated sensations. To be clear, I haven't lost *it* yet, to Ryan or anyone, for that matter. But that's not to say I don't think about it. Or want it. Dare I say, crave it.

Speaking of Ryan, the boy who stole my heart, the boy who wrote me pages of poetry recanting his punishing pangs of amour, the boy who challenged me to be me. And in doing that, he challenged me to challenge . . . us.

How, exactly?

That story, as it will play out over the next several months, culminating in an angsty armistice of bitter and sweet, is a little more complicated.

And so, on this Thursday night, hours after Andrew's weekly basketball game, minutes after saying good night to Ryan, Dustin and I share a sinful exchange of dirty dreams.

Friends do that, right?

"I have dreams about you naked," Dustin reveals matter-of-factly, and without the slightest hint of trepidation in his husky (hunky?) voice.

I have no idea how to be coy and sexy, which is how I want to come across. So I respond with, "Why?"

Nice, Sam.

"Because you're beautiful, smart, and have this really cute way of coming off totally innocent, yet highly sensual. It's a real turn-on."

Dustin is seventeen, a junior, and waaaaay more experienced than me. Which shouldn't be an issue for me, seeing as my boyfriend is approaching nineteen.

I realize I'm treading dangerously here. Honestly, it's out of sheer curiosity more than anything. I have no intention of cheating on Ryan. What constitutes cheating, anyway?

"Well, that sounds flattering," I acknowledge. "And a good note to end this conversation on. Have a good night, Dust—"

"Hold on," he interrupts my parting words. "You have nothing to say back?"

Clearly, he's disappointed. I probably would be too, if I were him.

"What is it you want me to say?" I'm getting pretty good at this double-talk game. How long before he figures it out?

"I'm not into the double-talk thing, Sam." He's stern.

That didn't take very long.

"Tell me something you like about me," he continues, softly this time.

"I think you're very handsome," I bark somewhat resentfully. "I think you have a biting humor that is repulsive yet alluring, and I don't know how I feel about it."

Too honest?

"See," he chides. "Was that so hard?"

Truthfully, it really was. It felt like I chugged Veritaserum and vomited niceties all over a boy who isn't my boyfriend.

"No, it wasn't. In fact, I've been waiting for an opportunity to share that with you since the day you returned Andrew's water bottle. I feel so much better now. What a relief."

I hear him smile over the phone, in the form of a pause indicative of upward curling lips.

"You'll probably sleep so good tonight, getting that off your chest," he offers.

I don't sleep at all. My mind somersaults between visions of Dustin touching my hip and coming in for a kiss.

On the other side of town, Ryan doesn't sleep either.

For different reasons.

Chapter 2

Sophomore year is one of those forgotten novelties of the high school experience. Last year, most things were new and exciting. Junior year, there's prom, (sanctioned) off-campus lunches, and grades matter a lot. Senior year, well, that's obvious.

Tenth grade is the bridge between underclassmenship and upperclassmenship. Most kids turn sixteen this year, which beckons the prospect of a driver's license, and with it, a car. Most kids who turn sixteen during the year show up to school the next day in their new ride. Our school parking lot looks something like a luxury car dealership.

For the Selim household, tenth grade represents the first time we will take the SATs, the first time we will take an AP class, the last time I will need to take second period dance class (so I have more periods to take classes that will *actually* help me get into college).

Sense a pattern here?

I managed to pull a set of straight As last semester, as if there was any doubt. There's something to the perfectionism of a 4.0 that I find oddly satisfying. Perhaps it's because I'm a perfectionist.

Ground-breaking conclusion.

Honestly, I've never gotten a B. I wonder what that would feel like. It's only a matter of time, I know. But I'd rather put it off as long as possible. The top colleges don't like Bs. At least, that's what I've been told in so many words by college counselors and Daddy, and these are the only opinions that matter.

I'm aware I'm being a tad dramatic. It's just that, when I commit to something, I *commit* to something. Exhibit A: my boyfriend.

We had a fun summer together. Lots of mornings at Blackies. Lots of movie dates followed by a trip to the bookstore. Lots of poems.

Like this one:

> We used to dance and sing all day,
>
> a couple kids making waves and catching rays.
>
> Cruising down the beach in your swanky Ford,
>
> belting out tunes—"whatchu waiting fooorrrrr"?
>
>
> You had your surfboard, I had my shades,
>
> the setting sun closed out our days.
>
> We chased hope like Obama preached
>
> out here, holding hands, on the beach.

He took me to the Surf and Sand in Laguna Beach for dinner one night, just cause. At least, that's what he said. Part of me thinks it was an affirmation attempt, an I-just-want-to-make-sure-you-still-love-me meal.

Kinda sweet, but also kinda unnecessary.

I'm not trying to be mean, or anything like that. I'm just not sure what it means.

There seems to be more of that in our relationship than I care to admit or be okay with.

Especially recently.

My priority has always been and will always be school, first and foremost. I've actually heard there are studies that show girls are better at balancing academics and personal stuff than boys. Anecdotally, I knew this one girl in elementary school—her brother was dating this other girl, and somehow he started flunking some of his classes while she, the gf, maintained straight As. Perhaps the differences in development across adolescent brains is the culprit.

It's science.

"Are you ready for your sophomore year?" Ryan asks me during the last week of summer break. I'm visiting him at his tower (if you could call it that) at 18 and Bay. There are a few spots on the bayside where the fire department stations lifeguards that supposedly have a "significant" number of beachgoers, enough to warrant the watchful eye of our trained water cavalry.

One time, Ryan noticed a dingy unhitch from its buoy and start floating away. As far as I know, that's the only rescue he's had while working an "and Bay" tower. All kidding aside, I understand the need for these posts, and fully support the efforts of our fire department in protecting our people and making sure our beaches stay safe and secure.

"I think so," I respond pensively. I'm semi-distracted by the to-do list of summer reading from each of my classes, mentally recounting the coursework and verifying completion. This summer, I had AP World History, French, and English (as ever) to prep for, with AP World requiring the most reading.

I love to read, but I never thought I would begin to resent it. My mom was a history major in college, with emphasis on American and Russian history. I imagine this choice was a reflection of the period she went to college, during the end of what we now call the Cold War.

It almost feels like the teacher assigned this much reading in an attempt to cover up what little he actually knows about the topic, so he can just direct us to "the reading" for the answers to our questions. Granted, World History is kinda a lot to cram into one school year, even with additional summer reading. There's also the issue with the point of view from which history is told.

I was in sixth grade when I started to learn about cultures outside the United States—and even then, it was about ancient civilizations, like Mesopotamia, Egypt, Greece, etc. Now, in tenth grade, is the first time I'm learning anything remotely detailed about current world affairs. How is it even possible to cram all of the world's history into eight months of study? Simple: it's not. The United States is not alone in prioritizing its country's history in school curriculums, and it makes sense for us to learn and understand the foundational truths upon which our country is built. However, it would behoove us, especially when it comes to understanding cultural diversity—arguably a foundational truth of our country as well—to prioritize learning about the world earlier and more often throughout our primary and secondary schooling years.

In kindergarten, we learned Christopher Columbus "discovered America" in 1492. But we didn't learn that Zheng He, an admiral from Ming dynasty China, landed in what is currently North America in 1421—about 70 years before Columbus. (There is controversy around this point as well, as the notion was first introduced in 2002 by Gavin Menzies titled *1421*.)

We also learned that Johannes Gutenberg invented the printing press in 1453. But we didn't learn that in 1050, the Chinese used ceramics to create movable type themselves—a full three centuries prior to Gutenberg.

From what I understand, school curriculums are being tweaked to account for our increasingly interconnected world and thus the knowledge we have about the world. The more aware we are of our world and what shapes it, the greater opportunity to have to shape it ourselves and make it better as best we can.

I digress.

Whatever the reasoning is, superfluous reading for the wrong reasons doesn't sit well with me.

Ryan's eyes are boring holes into my temples like he's digging into the darkest, deepest recesses of my brain's ridges at the slightest hope of finding something.

Despite knowing each other for the past year, these are his best efforts to understand what goes on in my head. To the best of my knowledge, it hasn't yielded the results he's hoping for. His glassy eyes betray his disappointment. Perhaps he should try an alternative approach. After all, the definition of insanity is doing the same thing over and over again expecting different results.

Ryan started school a few weeks ago. He's taking GE classes right now—I'm not sure which ones. He mentioned it to me once before, but I don't remember now.

"You think so?" Ryan asks, hardly hiding his exasperation with my lack of detail.

"I'll let you know tomorrow once I've recalibrated expectations with my teachers," I chide snidely before offering a peck of truce. To do this I have to climb three rungs of the so-called ladder to reach his cheek. He says he doesn't like when I do that because he could get in trouble with the unit supervisors for "having non-uniformed personnel in the tower."

I think he secretly loves it. So, I'm going off of that to inform my actions.

It's not like he tells me to stop.

"Sam, you know I could get in major trouble if someone saw you up here," he reprimands me.

He's actually serious.

My mistake.

I'm not, like, OTT mad, like I was after Prom last year. Even someone as nice as me entertains anger. (Ryan's brother Steven doesn't like me because he thinks I'm too nice, whatever that means.) I am disappointed, which honestly is probably worse. Anger can generally be assuaged. Disappointment requires a different kind of effort to overcome: trust. The cornerstone of every satisfying relationship, according to the actions of two archetypal movie characters, Jack Dawson and Aladdin. You know, when Jack helps Rose step up onto the railing of the speeding *Titanic*, and Aladdin invites Jasmine to see the world from the threads of a magic carpet?

What dreams may come.

Despite the wistful romanticism such cinema brings, the *real* stuff—the stuff that tests us and tips the scale towards hope or fear—needs more screen time.

If my life was a movie, it would be called "Love and Salt". Love, for the feelings that bind me to people, i.e. Ryan, in raw, redeeming ways. And salt, for the tingling pain that burns in open wounds, inflicted by betrayal and distrust—a deceptive version of fear.

I'm looking at Ryan, the boy I fell in love with, sitting on his tower, covered in sunscreen, eyes hidden behind Wayfarers. People show you who they are, but the hard part is believing what you see. Sometimes the mind plays games with your eyes, and the connection between the two is a highly trafficked thoroughfare of hopes, doubts, wishes, and cons. It's hard to see through the headlights.

I see a boy who wants to love, but who for some reason has issues. I mean, we all have issues. His issues, from my point of view, are rooted in insecurity. We're all insecure. We're teenagers. But these recurring lapses are getting on my nerves. *I'm supposed to be your person*. It's times like these I don't think he sees the value in that. And that part hurts.

And so, in my debilitating disappointment, I say, "Okay, I should get going anyways." I wrap my kashmari shawl around my hips and throw my water bottle and journal into my Aloha tote as quickly as possible—without trying to appear as if I'm trying to vacate the scene as quickly as possible.

"Sorry, Sam, I just don't want to cause any trouble."

Right, because getting a kiss from your girlfriend is SUCH a threat to beachgoer safety.

"It's okay."

It's not, but I don't have the patience or desire to have this conversation yet again.

"I'll call you later, babe," he calls to me from his wooden throne.

I smile, no teeth, a tell of mine that infers there are thoughts that remain hidden and unexposed between my ears.

Alas, Ryan does not know my tell, because he doesn't pay attention to such details. People show you who they are, but the hard part is believing what you see.

So I walk away towards my Electric cruiser, slightly annoyed, slightly hurt, and wholly unapologetic for my feelings.

I feel a buzzing reverberate in the pocket of my tote. I press the long button on the top right of my iPhone, illuminating my screen and revealing a text from Dustin.

Chapter 3

My heart leaps into my throat for a second before I can corral it back into the paddock of my rib cage.

I wasn't expecting to hear from Dustin, particularly in this moment, following a less-than-desirable exchange with someone who's supposed to be my other half.

Timing is everything.

I raise my phone towards my face to unlock it via recognition software. (How unreal is it that we live in a world where computers and AI and VR and whatever alphabet soup of technology can recognize our features, give us access to devices and other PII, all without the threat of fascist dictatorships taking over? Super scary.)

hi girlie, what r u up 2

He uses abbreviations whatever chance he gets. I wonder what that says about his personality? There's gotta be a thread on Reddit that speaks to this.

Just leaving the beach, you?

I, on the other hand, stray to the side of grammar and convention. I *will* shorten words and use all low caps most times, but I generally stick to a tight translation of what my voice would sound like when I converse in person, with my mouth.

Honestly, I'm still not totally grasping the whole "voice to text" revolution. I feel like it's yet another language we have to learn. You know how when you text (or Gchat or DM), you have a certain inflection or tone that is basically part of your identity? I feel like the same will be true of audio transcriptions.

Also, it's very possible I'm overthinking it. It's my internal anthropologist at work.

I'm sure I'll appreciate it more when I start driving and won't have to worry about texting on my phone while simultaneously holding onto the steering wheel.

*Nice. im reading The Lonely Buddha n
takin a break now*

thought of u

Great.

*The Lonely Buddhe made you think of
me?*

How flattering

actually

A pause of what seems like two whole minutes slithers by.

my mind wandered 2 u

that's not flattering?

Uh oh.

Why did your mind do that?

Classic aversion. A slightly upended version of double-talk.

bc I have dreams about you naked 😎

I saw that one coming from a mile and a dirty pun away.

*I don't see the cause and effect
correlation . . .*

He ignores my scholarly yet totally oblivious comment and continues.

> *n bc theres a mystery bout ya that*
> *gets me*
>
> *its very distracting*
>
> *it hurts my insides*

This is an awful lot of honesty (?) for a Thursday afternoon.

I hesitate, and decide a reply isn't my best move. A) because I don't know what to say, and B) he could use some intrigue.

What feels like hours cruise by. But really, it's the amount of time it takes me to ride my bike from 18th Street, home. Maybe ten minutes.

I check my phone after I tie up my bike inside the garage. Bikes get stolen, so yes, this precaution is necessary.

Nothing. Not a peep.

Clearly not everyone has my sense of urgency.

Daddy and I have that in common. We're the early risers, the better-now-than-later, Type A people. We can get frustrated easily as a result of it. Compared to Mama, Jenny, and Andrew, Daddy and I are the road runners, and the rest of our family are . . . not. It's nice to have an ally in him.

Sometimes my need for speed comes across as a need for power. Because I like to get things done quickly and efficiently, more often than not, I'm the one haranguing my counterparts for their glacial pace. I can see how that would be annoying. It's a point of contention in some of my relationships. Ryan is a lot like Mama, Jenny, and Andrew in that way.

I wouldn't say that I'm impatient—just that my baseline for time is inherently faster than others. I know there are other people out there that exist just like me and Daddy. I will meet more of them in the future. My people.

On the flip side, technically I should be the one replying, right? Texting etiquette these days stresses me out.

I close the garage door and head into the house through the back side of the kitchen. Mama is perched on the chair that makes up one half of the seats of her bistro set, reading the last bits of the *Wall Street Journal*. Mama basically curates news updates for our family so we aren't burdened/overloaded/overwhelmed by the ridiculous amount of updates making their way from the media through each of our devices—screen or otherwise. As someone who is a frequenter of rabbit holes, I fully support this approach, and use my rabbit-holing hours for more fulfilling activities like online shopping and watching TikTok videos.

Daddy is—you guessed it—in his favorite spot on his favorite couch, chin resting on his left hand as he looks towards the outside, lost in thought.

I see piles, nay, mounds of Andrew's friends' possessions scattered across the front patio. There's a good swell today, which is a cue for a dozen of Andrew's closest friends to invade Chez Selim.

The beach on this part of the peninsula faces towards the south, which basically means if there is a south swell, we get many visitors.

It took me a while to learn the difference between a wave and a swell.

Waves and swells are both generated by wind blowing over water. However, waves indicate the speed of the wind in that local area. Swells are waves that have moved beyond the area where they were generated. So, when a swell comes in, the waves we're seeing are the effects of a weather system that originated somewhere far away. Make sense?

Generally speaking, the spots where the waves will be biggest face toward the incoming swell. For example, a south swell that travels from south to north will be strongest at a break that faces either south or southwest. Hence the popularity of our spot. We should call it the Selim Swell, or Selim's Spot. It's got a nice ring to it.

Topography of a spot can also have some impact on surf quality. Sometimes, when we have a really big north or south swell, the breaks facing away from that swell may actually offer the cleanest and best surf, especially if you're not looking for huge waves. It depends on what you're looking for.

Andrew's friend Eddy calls my mom *every* morning during the summer to see what the waves are like. Surfline has cameras at The Wedge and The Point, but not at 11th Street. Thus, Mama is the de facto Wave Agent. She's gotten pretty good at it. She looks out from the balcony on the second floor and cobbles together a three-sentence summary describing the surf, using key phrases like 'glassy', 'choppy', and 'sets'.

I'm more of a land animal, myself. I've never been the strongest swimmer, but I do know how to tread and keep my head above water. There's a reason why I've never participated in JG's.

JG's is Newport's junior lifeguard program. For eight weeks in the summer, about 500 kids aged 10-15 participate in this program where they learn about ocean safety. There's swimming, some running, a pier jump (yikes!) and more swimming. It sounds like a surf and sand bootcamp to me, but my siblings love it.

Andrew and Jenny have both participated for the past few summers. There's a graduation and awards ceremony at the end, which essentially equates to a luau-ish BBQ. They show a video of footage recorded throughout the summer. I always find the music selection amusing. Whoever curates that content must have a good time.

This past summer, Andrew won what's called "The Instructor's Award." It's kind of like the teacher's pet of the group. We were all really surprised because, well, he would show up late a lot because he'd be bodysurfing.

Andrew and his friends were bodysurfing when the award itself was announced and presented during the ceremony. How appropriate and comically ironic.

His instructor wrote him a note saying how impressed he was with Andrew's bodysurfing skills. Andrew said my mom could keep his award. I think he was a little embarrassed. It was cute.

Ryan wants to be an instructor someday. He likes working with kids, and I think he'd be really good at it.

He might need to work on his sensitivity a little bit. The young ones are particularly impressionable. Hopefully he won't make them cry.

I feel a vibration as I lean in to give Daddy a kiss on the cheek.

"How was the beach?" he asks in his muted Punjabi accent.

"It was good, got some sun and went for a swim."

He gives me a questioning look.

"Don't worry, I stayed near the lifeguard."

Daddy doesn't know about Ryan. Still. He knows Ryan Peter Dayton, the person, exists. They met that one time last year on a Saturday following a surf. Daddy somewhat laid into him about his lack of academic inclinations. Boy didn't even notice, until I pointed it out to him.

He doesn't speak Ashar Selim.

I look at my phone, thinking it's Dustin.

It's not.

It's Ryan, apologizing with:

> *Sorry babe, didn't mean to be so*
> *fragile. Just been on edge lately.*
> *Forgive me?* 😔

Fragile indeed.

I consider his apology, thoughtful and introspective. Remorseful, yet explanatory.

> *Of course hunny, I forgive you.*

I catch myself wishing it was Dustin's name that had appeared on the screen.

Turning towards the staircase, I make my way towards my bedroom with every intention of hiding away until dinner time and burying myself in the next Great American Novel, *Midnight Sun*.

As I close the door to my room, my phone buzzes again. This time, it's a FaceTime call.

From Dustin.

Crap.

Be careful what you wish for.

Chapter 4

I totally chickened out and didn't answer the phone.
I texted him back twenty minutes later.

Hey, I'm with my family, call you later

Partially true.

Though I had no intention of calling him later.

His reply?

don't make me wait too long or else

That *kind of* sounds like a threat. Like he's on the precipice of a heist gone wrong, and I'm his last resort before he pulls the ill-fated trigger.

Duh; I know, in my rational mind, it's not that.

At this moment I'm predictably irrational. I'm sure Dan Ariely would be glad to write a case study about this scenario.

Texting By Teens Gone Awry Due To Overthinking.

I'm really bad at this flirting thing. It's probably my greatest flaw.

Besides my mediocre swimming abilities.

Obviously, reading is now out of the question. How many times have I reread the paragraph about the vampire's dewy eyes and the mystique of his aurora, cast like a mirror illuminating the windshield of his captor's ride?

Too many.

And so, instead of upping the intensity of this boundary-pushing-non-tryst with Dustin by indulging him in a video chat, I do the next best thing.

I daydream about upping the intensity of this boundary-pushing-non-tryst with Dustin by playing out multiple scenarios about what a video chat with him would look like.

Again, I am a rational actor.

In school we learn about philosophers who espouse that humans are rational creatures, that we make decisions based on logic over gut/intuition/feeling. Weber and Brandt clearly did not understand or seek to understand the behaviors of teenage girls.

We live in a world of *coulds* and *shoulds*, a basket of choices we (supposedly) use logic to make. Who determines these coulds and shoulds? In most cases I'd argue it's society, a concept in itself which is neither human or tangible. (It's a concept, and therefore inherently something we cannot see.) How ironic is that?

I digress.

What I'm saying is, clearly, the choices I'm making are not bolstered by logic but fanned by feeling. I have my reasons, but they aren't necessarily based on reason itself. I finally understand Spock's dilemma.

Ah, the complexities of a human (teenage) being.

After dinner, I toy with the idea of calling Dustin back. Or texting. Or emailing. Or messaging via courier pigeon. We have so many options to communicate these days, it's overwhelming. Paralysis by analysis is not uncommon, *especially* for this girl.

I go with texting. More control.

Now, what to say?

Hey? Hi? Sup?

Again, too many options.

I decide to go with a "hey there" and leave it open-ended.

Seconds later I receive the reply:

are you free to v-chat?

Yikes. So much for more control.

sure

I reply, against my better judgement.

Ok gimme a sec

His "sec" ends up being the longest three minutes of my life.

In that minute, I scurry—yes, scurry—frantically around my room, trying to find the best place to prop up my phone. The bookcase? Nah, then I'd have to stand the whole time, and I tend to shift my weight from foot to foot a lot. That could look weird on camera.

These are my problems. Confessions of a teenage, type A, (drama?) queen.

I settle on using my headboard, which acts like a nightstand that extends the width of my bed, aided by the lifetime set of my personal journals. When stacked, the top of these historical artifacts meets my gaze almost as if by divine destiny.

Perfect.

I throw on my favorite off-the-shoulder t-shirty blouse, a blush pink, paired with white shorts (not that he'll actually see anything below my waist, but it makes me feel confident). This choice screams *I made an effort but not too much.*

That's a mouthful for a wardrobe choice, but clothing designers know what they're doing. Call it fashion psychology.

My darker-than-olive skin glows against the gossamer fabric, my outer layer not quite finished absorbing the day's rays.

Phone propped, hair properly flipped and parted to the left, and pillow placed neatly under my bum for optimized posture, I wait for Dustin's call.

Not more than eight seconds pass before my screen lights up with the words *Dustin Peterson, Magic Maker . . . would like to FaceTime . . .*

Pausing for a few cleansing breaths, I plaster on a smile—out of nervousness more so than forced merriment—and answer with what I think is a sultry, "Hey . . ."

Chapter 5

OMG. That was intense.

Not to compare, but Ry would *never* be so shameless in his flirting as Dustin is. At least not with me.

Dustin, whose word choice is all but primal, straddles the boundary of playful and propositional.

Ry, well, he . . . doesn't. Not anymore, I don't think. Or maybe I just don't see it.

Adrenaline can have that effect on a brain. There's a cloudiness that shrouds your clarity, like a thunderstorm hovering on a horizon. The promise of lightning lingers, but it may or may not strike. It's hard to know because the bolts are buried within the eye, closed and unyielding. Like a secret. A tell-tale heart.

Tell-tale, like the fact that Ryan called me twice during my v-chat with Dustin, and I didn't want to answer.

I didn't want to talk to my boyfriend, but instead, to the boy masquerading as a friend who speaks to me in whispering tones—who has dreams about me naked.

What's wrong with this picture?

<h1 style="text-align:center">Chapter 6</h1>

*E*ventually, I call Ryan back.

Not immediately. First, I need some time to recover from whatever THAT was.

A few deep breaths and some downward-facing dog.

Moving on. Kind of.

"I was surprised you didn't pick up," Ryan comments.

What, so I'm always supposed to be available to you at all hours of the day?

I think it, but I don't say it.

To be honest, I genuinely don't believe he meant anything by it. I *usually* pick up on the first try. Nearly always. So, in a way, it is somewhat out of the ordinary for me to not be so responsive.

What is *also* out of the ordinary are these coy, coquettish conversations with Dustin.

"All good, babe, I just didn't hear the phone ring."

Which isn't untrue.

I didn't *hear* the phone ring. All I got were the banner notifications on my phone.

I speak the truth.

What is truth?

Socrates and I go way back. He describes truth as a journey with intention, guided by God or godlike intervention. While I cannot pick the brain of this father of the Socratic method to further understand his position, I also believe that truth is personal. These two ideas are not mutually exclusive. Perception is reality, an aspect of truth that we sometimes don't immediately recognize in our day to day. We could be looking at the same picture, and what I see is different from what someone else might see.

Like the viral blue/black versus white/gold dress illusion of 2015. Remember that?

Or like this image: 

Spoiler alert: this is both a younger woman and an older woman. What do you see?

We all see things differently.

Yes, I realize I may be trying to rationalize my response to Ryan.

But my point is still valid.

I digress.

"How was the rest of your shift?" I ask, hoping to change the subject.

"It was fine, quiet . . . " his voice trails off in a lapsing pause . . . "after you left."

Cool.

I let the pause linger in the air for a heavy moment, plump and swollen like a fat lip after a fist fight. Only the silent sting of salt can cure this cut.

Ryan has never been comfortable with silence. He's a talker, like one of those tech salesmen that convinces you that you need this app or that upgrade, even though you know you'll never use it. So you let him talk anyway, because he's going to reveal his spiel regardless of whether you interrupt him or not. Ultimately, it will be quicker than pausing for side conversations that he doesn't care about, because his ultimate goal is to get a sale—i.e., convince you that you need whatever he's proposing for you.

Not that Ryan has to sell me on his love. Love isn't the question. It's the salt—the grains of crystal that taste bitter and dry, yet contain healing powers. As with most things, moderation is key. Too much salt makes your food taste like cement, and too much love makes your relationship feel like a scuba diver in an underwater cage: breathing, alive, and adrenaline-pumping, but in the end, still trapped.

"At least you didn't have any distractions?" I offer, with a hint of forced pep that even I have a hard time faking.

"Right, yeah, that's true." His voice is almost a whimper, deflated, like a flat tire.

"What's wrong?" I ask. I can't help myself. *Someone* needs to say *something*.

"I'm not exactly sure," Ryan begins. "Things just feel . . . I don't know . . . *different*, between us."

Great.

"Different how?" Seems like the next logical question in this sequence of discovery.

"It feels like you're being distant," he says flatly, not accusatory but more like a statement of fact than a thoughtful consideration. I would have preferred the latter.

Inside I seethe, like a slow-burning stove jouleing out heat.

Outside, I take a deep breath and, as calmly as I can, make my best attempt to understand his observation.

"I see. Can you explain what you mean by 'distant', and some times that you've felt this way?"

"Why are you doing that?"

Okay, not what I expected him to say.

"Doing what?"

"Talking about our relationship like you're talking about the weather."

"Excuse me?"

"It's like you don't even care. It doesn't even feel like you're concerned or care about what I think, or how I'm feeling."

Someone's projecting.

"Hold on a second, you're mad because I'm NOT going off on you like a broken firecracker and fueling the fire? Do you realize how crazy that sounds?"

I can hear his fumes through the phone, a bull ready to rush Pamploma.

"Well—"

"For the record, I'm not the one who's upset or hurt or angry. That's you right now. And I'm trying to understand why you feel this way. Because I can't control your feelings; only you can do that. What I'm trying to do is understand what the root cause is so we can fix it. So forgive me if it sounds like I'm talking about the weather."

More silence hangs, longer this time. For a minute I think he hangs up the phone, but his sniffles betray his presence. I swear this guy cries more than I do.

I'm all for a good emote, but his timing could be better.

Eventually, he speaks.

"Just forget it, I'm not mad. I've gotta go shower. I'll text you later."

The most staccato of exits if I've ever heard one.

And with that, our conversation is over, a classic runaway train.

I let the silence envelop me for a moment. All I can hear is the sound of my own breath.

I'm not mad, either. Disappointed, sure. Let's be real—we've had a lot of disappointing moments for one day.

Maybe we just need space.

Yeah, space.

Maybe time, too.

Chapter 7

We have the same fight over and over again. Like after Prom last year, about the whole insecurity thing, when he straight-up lied about why we left the afterparty and put it on me.

(He told the host I was tired and wanted to leave, when in fact it was he who was tired and wanted to leave.)

Like, why can't you own it?

So I'm trying to understand where these feelings come from, so we can at least talk about them and figure out how we can make it better.

But then I get accused of approaching it like a weather report.

Dustin is a whole other set of seasons to figure out.

He has a Philistine flare to him—simple, yet layered in mystery. Maybe that's just my interpretation from where I stand.

They are totally unique and separate parts of my life, compartmentalized and un-entwining. Is that wrong?

I am the link, unbeknownst to them. They don't even know the other exists. Like a six degrees of separation where the Kevin Bacon connection remains anonymous.

Tricky.

Chapter 8

Ryan and I make up. As usual.

This reconciliation feels more like a doormat greeting, templated and cozy.

He initiates it, which I appreciate. Also as usual, I don't believe I did anything wrong.

And so we move on.

School starts today, and I'm semi-dreading it.

Ryan won't be there, my college-aged catch. As such, I have no friends to hang out with.

I realize this is partially my own doing.

Since my falling out with Alex and Charlie last summer, my efforts to build new female friendships have been virtually nonexistent.

I tried calling this other girl, Lucie, about a last-minute question on some AP World History summer assignment. It's true I had never called her before for anything remotely friendly.

Let's just say it's clear where her allegiances lie.

I don't blame her.

At the same time, it feels a little mean-girl-ish. Rational or not, this teen girl thing is not as fun as it seems on "All-American". Though the drama rivals real life.

Day one is fine. Just fine. As expected, my existence brims on cursory amongst the FGP ("former gal pal") group.

Walking onto campus from the pool parking lot, I see them congregating near the planter we claimed as our hangout spot during our middle school days.

Good thing I'm wearing my latest confidence-boosting outfit: a deep purple knee-length skater dress with nude flats.

One day last year, some punk wrote "Big Tits" on my locker in black Sharpie. I was mortified. I went home feeling like an elephant had sat on my sternum and wouldn't get off until the locker was clean. The next morning, we got to school super early and I repaired the damage with a teaspoon of Comet bleach and a sponge. The bleach may have taken off a coat of paint along with the offending script, but I was satisfied.

This was early in the year before Ryan and I started hanging out, something like the second week of school. I've done my best to block out the memory, but despite my best efforts, it lies dormant covered in cobwebs in the dusty depths of my brain. I'm still not sure who actually did it, but I have a list of suspects. I'm convinced it was the kid with the locker below mine. He's a year older than me. I don't know his name.

I will never understand what writing something like that on a fifteen-year-old's locker will accomplish.

It's not clever. It's not cunning. It's definitely not cute.

Obviously I won't let some horny teenager influence my wardrobe choice. But I'm still allowed to feel embarrassed by such incidents. I just can't let them—people, or my feelings—control my own behavior.

I digress.

First up is AP World History. First period classes are the worst—regardless of the subject matter—because no one has had the class yet, and therefore can't tell you what to expect. By breaktime there's usually some buzz around the contents of periods 1 and 2, especially on a test day or major assignment due date. The best days are when something gets canceled in a class you don't have until after lunch, and you hear about it before 10 a.m. The planner in me appreciates these kinds of heads-up.

The teacher for APW is a former Olympian-turned-author, turned-high school teacher. I think he met his wife during the summer games in Atlanta in 1996, but don't quote me on it. I'm not sure exactly how much he knows about the history of the world, which really, I don't really care about. I just want to get a good score.

For AP exams, which happen over the course of two weeks in May, passing scores include 3, 4, or 5—5 being the highest. Obviously I'd love to get a 5—who wouldn't? But seeing as it's my first go-around on the AP train, I won't be devastated if I don't.

I can hear Daddy's voice in the back of my mind, chanting, "5, 5, 5, 5 . . . "

Not really, but you get the idea. The expectations are there.

The teacher's name is Mr. Dean. He carries himself with a confidence only athletes can muster, the confidence in their mental and physical capabilities.

"Welcome back to class," he booms from the front of the class. "I trust you've completed your summer reading? Because that's where we're starting. But first, let me tell you about myself . . . "

Which ends up taking the balance of the class period. After the bell rings, he concludes with, "We'll pick this up tomorrow."

Next up is Algebra II.

I like equations and stuff. But today, I spend most of the class thinking about what to do during break. And even worse, lunch. A whole thirty-five minutes of queasy chaos churning inside my brain.

Since I have no friends.

I could go to the library—that's my first thought. But why would I need to go to the library on the first day of school? I'm desperate, but not that desperate. I can't wait until I can drive; then I can just sit in the car and pretend to be on my phone, talking to "friends that don't go to school here." I'll be sixteen in seven months. I guess I can wait that long.

Assuming Daddy will let me drive the car.

I have really good supporting arguments for my position. I could drive Jenny AND Andrew to school. That would free up hours for Mama to do what she does, which would also save on fuel costs AND be better for the environment overall. Carbon footprints need to be substantially reduced in my lifetime if we're going to survive as a species.

Maybe I should be a lawyer.

Maybe there are some new kids I can befriend? But I don't want to come on too strong, seeing as it's the first day and all.

And so I float through the day, keeping to myself and finding ways to wander around campus. I hope nobody notices my ambulatory patterns. I think to call Ryan, but I don't want to appear weak in his eyes. I'm a tough girl.

So tough that when I walk into sixth period English, I almost run over someone who looks the size of a hockey player.

Turns out, he *is* a hockey player.

More on him later.

Chapter 9

My phone lights up with Ryan's face as I open the door to the car. The first day is over, and Mama makes the second of her daily dual rounds to school to pick us up.

To reiterate, I could be so helpful to her—alleviate so many frustrating left turns (there are three on our route)—and most of all, save her time. Putting a pin in that thread.

I feel a sense of relief as I answer the phone. Ah, a familiar feeling. One of safety and comfort. Hello, my old friend.

"Hey babe!" Ryan practically shouts, way too jubilantly for three o'clock in the afternoon. "How was your first day back?"

"Oh, ya know how first days go . . . much ado about nothing . . ."

Sometimes I quote Shakespeare to see if he catches on. Most of the time he doesn't, which is okay. It's more of a game I play with myself.

That sounds weird, but it is what it is. I enjoy it.

"What does 'ado' mean?"

One of the things I like about Ryan is his extensive vocabulary. And by extensive, I mean it's bigger than most people I know, including adults. I think it's cute when he takes the initiative to expand it even more so.

Take away: always keep growing.

I don't even know what 'ado' means, technically; but that's not the point, so I make it up and assume I'm right. Fake it till you make it.

"Fanfare, debauchery . . . your favorite word!" I tease, kind of.

Debauchery really is his favorite word.

"Har har," he mocks, obviously in jest. "You're so funny I forgot to laugh!"

"In all seriousness," I continue, ready to move this conversation forward, "it was as expected. Nothing earth-shattering to report. How was class?"

I decide it best not to mention that I ate lunch—sliced green apples, woven wheats, and sliced gouda—in the back corner of the library amidst the presence of poets like Rupi Kaur and Silvia Plath. Not a good time.

"Didn't have class today," Ryan reports, "it got canceled because the professor was sick."

Ah, college life.

So I *could* have texted him to rescue me. Mental note: if you don't ask, the answer is always no.

Loosely translated: even if your boyfriend has a scheduled class, you should still ask if he can save you from eating lunch in the library like an outcast.

"Wow, a free day! What did you do?"

My money is on surfing.

"Went for a surf, it was low key. Crazy how empty the lineup is in the middle of the day."

The lineup is just what it sounds like—the spot off shore where surfers wait for their waves to roll in.

"Must be nice," I flippantly reply, not meaning to sound jealous or unhappy for him and his stress-free session of south swell happiness.

Continuing before he can say something about it, I say, "I'm just leaving school, I'll call you later tonight?"

"Sounds good babe, just text me."

One of the things I don't like about Ryan is when it comes to communicating, he prefers texting to calling.

It may sound like a little thing—and yes, true, he did just call me—but it's a big pain when I just want to have a convo that doesn't require a type delay and backlighting. I can already feel my retinas burning out because of the blue light. Plus, all the bings and bangs—or whatever the onomatopoeic words are for alerts—make me dizzy as I'm checking my phone every five seconds. It's like these tech companies know how to exacerbate teenage FOMO to the nth degree.

I just want to have a regular conversation with my boyfriend, like Sandy and Danny, or Bonnie and Clyde.

"Kay, bye," is all I can muster. As I sigh a great sigh, one that sounds like an exhale after the naggiest of namastes, I see Mama flicker her glance away from my direction.

"What, Mama?"

"Oh, nothing dear, just wanted to make sure you were all the way in the car before I drive away."

Smooth. Now I feel like an ass.

I stew in silence the rest of the way home, feeling guilty for snapping at my mom and feeling resentful of Ryan's preferences of conversation medium. Not to mention, I'm feeling phony for my lack of communication. Which is ironic, since I'm super chatty by nature. So it feels wrong

There is danger in duplicity.

Chapter 10

I didn't mention that Dustin sent me a few choice texts throughout the day. Not to Ryan. Not to Mama. Not to anyone.

Except to the kid in my English class.

Remember him?

His name is Mark.

It was an accident, really. I was putting my phone away, into the outer pocket of my vintagey backpack, when it slid off the patent leather and onto the floor. Mark, my new neighbor to the south, picked it off the ground *just* as Dustin sent me a message about a random thread he saw on Reddit.

He's still saved as *Dustin Peterson, Magic Maker* in my phone.

Mark took one look at the screen and released the deepest guttural laugh I've heard in a while. Something like a garbage disposal gurgling yesterday's dregs.

For a split second his face betrayed a hint of sheepishness, before regaining his status quo composure. Quomposure? That could be a song title.

"I think the magic maker is looking for a new act." He smiles devilishly as he hands, or rather tosses, my phone into my open palm.

"I personally think he still needs help with pulling a rabbit out of his ass, but I'll confirm and let you know."

He looks slightly affronted at my reply—I can't tell if it's shock, curiosity, maybe a little of both?

After a lapse of sideways glances, he smiles and extends his hand, seemingly in peace.

"I'm Mark, and you are . . . "

"Mischief Maker," I offer coyly as I accept his gesture of truce. "But my given name is Samantha."

He laughs again, softer this time, wearing a smirk.

"Nice to meet you, Sammy. Okay if I call you Sammy?"

"They all do."

"Who's they?"

"Wouldn't you like to know . . . "

Chapter 11

I text Ryan after dinner, against my better judgement. I think I just want to cut him some slack and see if he can prove me wrong.

We still haven't had the "serious talk" about our relationship and addressed the little spats we've had.

They're not even spats! They're little annoyances that sneak up in conversation disguised as spats. Like devils wearing halos who call themselves angels.

Hey you up?

It's 7:30, after *Jeopardy!*.

Call it corny humor.

Just studying for a math test

Eeek. That doesn't sound promising. Math was never Ryan's strong suit. But it's nice to see he's putting the effort in. There was a time PS (pre-Sam), i.e., when he was a junior in high school, that he decided not to take math past Algebra 2. I'm supportive of this development.

> *Aw ok. I'll leave you alone
> then.maybe we can have a date night
> this weekend?*

It feels like it's been ages since we've gone on a date. Year one of our romance was riddled with random jaunts to the ice cream shop, book store, and local juicery Qwench. (We started cheating on Dez and I kinda feel bad about it.) Plus, I think we need an excuse to be . . . alone together.

> *Can't this weekend babe. It's Bree's
> cotillion on Saturday . . .*

That's right. I'd forgotten alllll about it. Or subconsciously locked it into the deep, dark dungeons of my mind.

Bree is Ryan's childhood friend. SHE is Ryan's childhood friend. They took baths together. They grew up going to church together. Their parents are really close.

Over the summer, I found out Bree's cotillion debutante charity league coming-out-party thing (is it still called that?) is this year. Not to be confused with the "coming out of the closet" life event that LGBTQ people experience. Apparently it was decided a long time ago that Ry would be her escort. Personally, I love to dance and dress up, so the idea of choreographed dancing and beautiful white dresses resonates with me. I'm still not sure, though, how I feel about the idea of "coming out" in the introducing a woman to society kind of way. I don't think the actual act has the same meaning as it used to. It's very *Pride and Prejudice,* which is sort of old English glam and idyllic at the same time. The institution itself is old, which may be reason alone to icks-nay the practice altogether, because despite people's best intentions, it's hard to purge practices of their legacies. Or maybe it just needs a rebrand.

I remember really wanting to take cotillion classes when I was a kid. The whole thing seemed so theatrical, like a performance, scripted down to cutlery and foot placements. That's the part that appealed to me, not the "coming out" part. Lots of rituals are like this, like prom. There's histories that sometimes we'd prefer to forget. Sometimes it's better to cut all ties. Sometimes it's better to revamp and renew.

We all have choices to make.

I digress.

It's not that I have a problem with Ryan being Bree's escort. Please. It's not like I think he'd cheat on me with her, or with anyone, for that matter.

What I don't appreciate is how he didn't even *pretend* to care about what I thought about it, or attempt to secure my okay.

THAT I have a problem with.

Obviously I wouldn't put up a big stink and create some sort of irrational claim that he doesn't care about my feelings. The irony is that, had there been some remote effort to placate my ego, we wouldn't have gotten into this tiff in the first place.

What does that tell you?

It tells me he's either bad at confrontation (which we've seen) or he's keeping more secrets that I'm not yet privy to. Or, all of the above.

Sadly, I'm inclined to think it's all of the above.

What does that tell me?

I simply respond with:

That's right, that will be fun.

After a few minutes go by, I realize the conversation is over and we won't speak again until tomorrow.

Chapter 12

"**H**ow's the magic maker?"

I turn around only to be confronted by Mark's stupid grin, not inches away from my tight-lipped face.

Is it really going to be *that* kind of sixth period today?

It's my last class on a Friday, and this beefy buttercup wants to incite me. Just what I need.

After the briefest of pauses—mostly for effect—I reply, "Managing his mischief."

"Expecto patronum to you too, Sammy."

Huh. I'm mildly impressed.

Shifting gears, I transition the conversation away from the murky depths of my exploration with Dustin to a safer topic, like homework.

"Did you finish the reading assignment?" I ask in my doe-eyed innocence. My fingers perch over the back of my chair like talons on a tree branch. My feet remain hitched to the carpet in perpendicular geometry under my desk so that my torso stretches itself, like a reverse-warrior pose in yoga.

My practice has been progressing. The meditation part is taking me a while to master, but I'm happy to report progress.

For example, when Jenny takes my boar hair brush from my room without asking me, I let it go. I take a deep breath, release the frustration in my exhale, and most importantly, move on.

Before, I would make my peeve-y-ness known and verbally accost her until I was content with the impact. Obviously, this still happens and will continue to happen. I'm only human. But it is an improvement. Baby steps.

"I skimmed the SparkNotes," Mark replies. "Got the key plot points down."

Figured as much. Not the studious type.

"Do you read?" I sound accusatory and suspect, like I'm cross-examining a witness who ran a stop sign in traffic court.

"Doesn't skimming include some level of literacy?" he coyly tells more than asks.

"Some level," I acknowledge, accompanied by the token rolling of my hazel eyes.

"You're kinda funny," Mark states pointedly and without consternation. "Good wit."

"Good wit?" That's rich. "It sounds like you're complimenting a body part."

"I could do that too, but I'll leave that to the Magic Maker."

If only he knew.

Chapter 13

Last night, Andrew had a game. We saw each other, Dustin and I, offering knowing nods of hello from across the gym. IYKYK.

Which leaves the two of us as the only possible outers.

We haven't *talked* talked in a while. Honestly, I'm not sure I'm really into it anymore. He makes me uncomfortable—not in a bad, unsafe, overzealous way though, if that makes sense. In the *life begins at the edge of your comfort zone* kind of way.

Not to mention he's done wonders for my ego. I don't overlook that contribution in the least bit.

What does that say about my relationship with Ryan?

Ryan, who took me to lunch today because he wanted to do "something" with me before the weekend officially begins, since he'll be tied up in debutante commitments?

All he has to do is show up, but maybe that's just me.

Not to belittle the gesture. He's full of gestures. Remember how we first started dating? The flower-gram? I was SO embarrassed at the time, but I definitely appreciated the thought. I especially love how he curates Spotify playlists for me as gifts. My (former) friends thought this to be cheap. How dare they? Like I expect him to buy me diamonds, even if he does live in the 92663 zip code.

I will say, though, he does have a different relationship with money than me. It's a sensitive topic, especially in this capitalistic society we live in. Especially in this red pocket in a blue state. I'm most definitely not in a position to offer any sort of guidance for how the world can fix its socioeconomic problems, but I do think all people can better educate themselves and empower others.

I usually pay for my own meals, meaning I use my allowance. At the beginning, this admittedly kind of bothered me. For whatever reason (maybe influenced by Disney) I always thought it was a sign of chivalry for the courter to pay. I guess he's not technically courting me anymore, so we're past that. That concept is somewhat archaic in any case. Chivalry (knights and stuff) and other non-European concepts similar to it (i.e. samurai bushido) existed during a time when women produced limited economic value. Gender roles were siloed, and women mainly baked buns in their metaphorical ovens in addition to overseeing the equivalent of a household. Women didn't have the opportunity to earn a dollar, yen, or peso like we do today. It's barely been 100 years since female citizens of the US have had the right to vote! It sounds like a substantial amount of time, but really, it's just a sneeze in the history of the world. Vatican City is technically the last place in the world that still prohibits women from voting. Even so, it is still difficult for women in other countries to vote, despite their legal ability.

My point being, I feel like a hypocrite wanting my boyfriend to pay for my meals when I can do it myself, while some women can't even cast a ballot for their next local official. (I technically can't either, but I will be able to in about two years.) I have the power to spend, yet they don't have a voice. Not apples to apples, but you see the parallels.

Bringing it back to women as commodities rather than buyers and sellers of commodities. Kind of like a metaphor for debutante balls.

It always comes full circle.

Chapter 14

On Sunday morning, the fam bam and I take Mama out for a bountiful birthday brunch at the local IHOP.

This IHOP, which sits across the street from John Wayne Airport, is the former site of Moonraker. Moonraker is one of my mom's old haunts from her brokering days. Once a manager of a national trading firm's local office (girl power!), Mama would eat lunch every day at this Moonraker while collecting her margin calls. I swear, every time she speaks of her commodity managing days, this establishment finds its way into the conversation.

Flanked in fondness. Sprinkled in nostalgia. Soaked in sanctity.

I'm sure Daddy dined with Mama a time or two at this Moonraker. He doesn't detail the chronology of their courtship like Mama does.

He does, though, say things like, "Your mom is a good woman."

We all have our tells, our characteristic cues that make us who we are. One of Daddy's is his concise use of words to describe the things he loves. He never explicitly uses the word "love"—that's an Indian thing.

It's almost like saying the word devalues it somehow. It sounds kind of silly; I tell my Mom I love her at least twenty times a day, as a sign of affection or as parting words.

Personal preference, I guess.

Ryan says "I love you" a lot, too.

Sometimes I feel like *he feels* we have to say it at the close of every conversation, that it means something if we don't.

Which, if I'm being honest, it probably does.

Another kind of cue.

For example, I haven't heard from Ryan since before his call time at the country club yesterday.

That's a tell if I've ever seen one.

Chapter 15

After brunch, we—the sibs and I—hit the beach.

Meaning, I soak up some rays while Jenny and Andrew skim the waves.

September in Newport is our Indian Summer. The air is still hot and heavy with moisture that hangs like dangly earrings. But the beaches are empty, save for local folk and college kids on the quarter system.

I purposely leave my phone at home in an attempt at a digital detox. I usually end up on Instagram and spend more time than less capturing content for my story. They often consist of a well-composed shot of my beach towel/sari, Hydro Flask covered in stickers from Hawaii, a token beach read, and a peek of the ocean somewhere in the background.

That's my staple image. Please don't steal it.

I have to weigh the cost/benefit of removing the option for audio, i.e. a soundtrack playlist or podcast.

Today, my thoughts are enough to narrate my nap on the shoreline.

Or lack thereof.

Who am I kidding?

I'm peeved. ALL CAPS PEEVED. My thoughts weave between who Ryan talked to and danced with and flirted with. A sinking feeling in my stomach comes and goes, like a boomerang with a motor. The *Titanic* has nothing on me.

Yes, I realize I can't control how he behaves. Sound logic. Yet this feeling blows through my belly as though it's a tumbleweed cruising through a one-horse town. Then comes back again. And again. An unwanted yet deeply troubling feeling parked in Teenage Town at the corner of Hope and Fear. Hopeful that he's practicing his preach of love, yet fearful he's treading, dare I say crossing, the boundary into unfaithfulness.

I should talk, right?

It doesn't feel like the same thing, at least not to me.

In yoga, we set intentions for each class. In my journal practice, I record intentions every day. I have no intention of cheating on my boyfriend.

I don't know if I could say the same for him.

It's not an issue of trust, no—that's not it.

It's more about his relationship with himself, about his own confidence. I can't control that.

As Jenny would say, "That sounds like a *you* problem."

Before I know it, it's almost three in the afternoon. I wake up from whatever I was doing for the last few hours, laying face down, to the shock of salty seawater pooling on my back.

Apparently Andrew thought it funny to dump the leftover salt water from his fins onto my back.

We used to call him *Andy* when he was a baby. Daddy insisted that when he turned 5, we start calling him *Andrew*, because *Andy* is a baby name. Supposedly.

At ten, he hasn't gotten his height yet. But he can throw a helicopter in a barrel like the best of them.

Basketball season is nearly over, and Dustin will no longer be his coach.

When I get home, I'm greeted by six missed calls and ten texts.

All from Ryan.

Did somebody die? Where's the fire?

Turns out he just wanted to make sure *I* was okay.

Ooooookay.

You know how I said I was peeved?

I changed my mind.

I am indifferent.

Which, to be honest, is way worse.

Chapter 16

He had a nice time at the party, he shares. Other than the tux-and-tails ensemble he was required to wear, it was a good time.

Admittedly, I tune out the rest of the conversation.

Which segues into tentative plans to hang out this week and maybe visit a pumpkin patch since it's fall now. Though it still feels like summer.

And ends, of course, with the required *I love you* sign-off.

I say it back.

Chapter 17

I started tutoring this kid named Todd. I had signed up to be a part of AMP, or Academic Mentoring Program, at the beginning of the year. I don't get paid or anything, but I do get credit towards my community service hours. We're supposed to have at least forty over our high school careers to graduate.

He doesn't talk much, Todd. We've had a few sessions so far. Math needs the most help, according to him.

"I'm not great in geometry," he concedes. "The triangles confuse me." So honest.

"Triangles can definitely be confusing. You're not alone there. Let's start with some basics, then we can see where we need to focus our time. Is that okay with you?"

"Sure." Monosyllabic. Nice. Apparently it's not just how my brother communicates. Affirmations across the board are indicative of truth.

After a few half-hour sessions, he's starting to get it. He gets a B on his most recent test—a humble improvement from his last C+.

Then he hits me with it.

"Would you want to get food with me sometime?" He stutters slightly and doesn't make eye contact. "And, umm, not study?"

It takes me a minute to translate this proposition. I'm kinda caught off guard. I guess I assumed that most people know I have a boyfriend. But then again, Ryan doesn't go to school here anymore, and it's not like I flaunt it. I guess you wouldn't know unless you saw us together when Ryan picks me up or drops me off at lunchtime. And for good rule-abiding citizens like Todd, the parking lot is not a place one frequents, seeing as leaving campus is off limits to underclassmen.

After the stun wears off—over a period of about five seconds— I recover from my shock. "That's really nice, Todd, but I have a boyfriend. I don't think that would be fair. But thank you."

"Oh, shit, sorry—I didn't know—" He's flummoxed, overwhelmingly flummoxed. "This is awkward. You probably don't want to tutor me anymore, huh . . ."

That went from zero to one hundred really quickly.

"Don't worry, Todd. Awkward is a mindset. This is not awkward, trust me. Nothing happened. We're just talking."

"Wow, uh, okay." He seems relieved. Pausing for a moment, he looks at me, asking for permission to continue. When I wait for him to continue, I'm met with, "You're really mature."

Yeah. Tell me something I don't know.

"Thank you for the compliment," is what I say instead. "Now, about the isosceles . . ."

Chapter 18

I think I figured out my routine for how to spend my break and lunchtimes, a whole fifty minutes plus passing periods to fill.

It's almost Thanksgiving. After some trial and error, I came up with something that works for me.

On most days.

During break, I linger at my locker for as long as possible before making my way towards the library. I don't actually go *in* the library until lunch time.

There are tables and chairs that border the perimeter of the glass that cases the entrance to the library. I don't like to sit there because it's too easy to make eye contact with passersby. Too much potential for judgement.

I like to sit in these cubby-like units that look like phone booths with chairs. (I know, people used to make phone calls in tiny rooms before cell phones were a thing. Life must've been simpler then.)

The privacy is nice, and eye contact is all but impossible.

Usually I'll get started on homework or review if I have a test later in the day. Every minute helps, I tell myself.

During lunch, I read and hide in the back corner of the library, amidst the book stacks. I sit with my back towards the entrance so, you know, eye contact doesn't happen.

Sometimes this other kid—I think he's a junior?—gets to my spot before me, so I have to sit somewhere else that doesn't allow for the solitude I seek.

Technically, we're not supposed to eat in the library. Seems kinda silly to me. I don't eat a lot anyways. I usually snack on my default cheese and crackers, or a tuna sandwich if, in the morning, I anticipate I'll be hungry.

And sometimes, Ryan takes me out to lunch.

Sometimes, though, I wish I had a friend group.

As I'm leaving the stacks, I notice a flyer on the windowed entrance to the hallway. It has a pitchfork on it. Weird.

Getting closer, I see it's not a pitchfork. It's a harpoon.

Harpoon. The school magazine.

The next issue is coming out soon and the staff is soliciting ideas for features from the students. How inclusive.

What about a feature on library science? I would read it.

Chapter 19

*L*ife is so unpredictable, like the best weather forecast. While the most skilled meteorologists do their best to project weather formations using their top-notch tools, even they're wrong sometimes. Mother Nature is an independent woman and will not be chained to expectation, no matter how informed.

Apparently, so is Alex.

Apart from ignoring each other during the passing period between 3rd and 4th, we haven't acknowledged the other's existence since The Great Schism. At least I haven't. Probably out of self-preservation more than anything. I have no interest in revisiting that feeling I had when I approached my "friends" on a typical morning before class, and they walked away as if I smelled like the inside of a barn that hadn't been cleaned in weeks.

When I see either Alex or Charlie, my stomach expands and pushes up against the base of my heart, causing my insides to contract like they do when I'm on my period. And it hurts.

I am tough when necessary, but really, I am more sensitive than babies are to light when they first enter the world.

You can imagine my surprise when she came up to me at my locker during break, *on purpose*.

She could have texted me if she wanted, but she sought me out, *in person*. That gesture alone is worth noting.

"Hey," she begins, somewhat garish in tone but inviting all the same. "What's up?"

Direct and to the point.

"Good," I reply, equally generic and enthusiastic. Tit for tat.

"Good," she follows.

We're on a roll, here.

"So," she continues, cutting to the chase. "I'm having a boat parade party in a few weeks, and wanted to ask if you wanted to come."

Oh. That's unexpected.

Before I can respond, she pulls out what appears to be an invitation from her back pocket. It's about the size of a postcard. On it are the details of the fête: date, time, location, RSVP details. In the background is a photo of a yacht decked out in holiday decor, a Santa posted at the helm supposedly manning the boat.

My attempt at producing words using my mouth is paltry at best. My brain is so stunned at what's happening physically that it can't compute language.

Paralysis by analysis.

Alex extends her hand, the invitation hovering between us like a floating feather suspended on a gentle breeze.

My fingers, likely out of impulse, accept the offering.

I manage a "Thank you, Alex," but I'm not sure if she hears me.

I'm not sure if *I* hear me.

She smiles delicately. I swear I see her eyes light up..

I'm left standing there, looking down at the silky cardboard between my hands. A Shutterfly product, no less.

I'm not sure what that was.

Whatever it is, it's something.

Didn't see that coming.

I'll just blame it on the weatherman.

Chapter 20

This seems like the year of Indian and Indian American programming* on Netflix. (Or maybe my feed is just curated like that?) Over the past few months, I've watched "Never Have I Ever" and "Indian Matchmaking." I don't usually watch a lot of TV, aside from Jeopardy! with my family. But these pieces of content have been welcome distractions from my . . . personal matters. My observations:

1. Never have I ever heard the word "jolly" used so much.

2. Differentiating a *love marriage* and an *arranged marriage*, or I guess more so the terms themselves, seems like an all or nothing proposition. Why can't an arranged marriage also be for love, or vice versa?

3. Mindy Kaling makes me laugh really hard.

4. Judgement and bias are not unique to any one group or culture. One of the matchmaking participants was told she wasn't considered a "real Indian" because she was born in

Guyana (South America) and not India proper, even though both her parents are ethnically Indian. I don't get that. (Furthermore, what does that make me?)

5.   I never knew there was such a thing as sikh camp.

*PSA: It's important to remember these programs are forms of entertainment and should not be regarded as the final word on Indian or any other culture.

<h1 style="text-align:center">Chapter 21</h1>

Alex's dad has a place on Lido Isle, on the northwest side, kitty corner to restaurant row on Pacific Coast Highway, a.k.a. PCH, a.k.a., prime Boat Parade viewing real estate. His ambulance business has provided for a lifestyle that affords such purchasing power.

There's a lot of money in Newport Beach. This is no secret. Last I checked one of it's zip codes, 92657 (Newport Coast) is the 24th most expensive zip code in the country. There's inherited money and self-made money, like anywhere else.

My parents, with their entrepreneurial aptitudes, made their money over years of analyzing the markets. Years and years. I'm not an economist, but they have the minds that see these opportunities.

My dad's dad (my *daadaa*) wanted him to be a doctor, a medical doctor. What a missed opportunity that would be. From what I understand, it's a cultural thing. Doctor, lawyer, pharmacist. Master of the markets doesn't exactly fall into one of those buckets, as far as his parents were concerned.

Me, I'm a more creative sort of person. Not the kind of person that enjoys statistics and spreadsheets, but the kind that enjoys words and colors and composition. Thankfully, the focus right now is on education, not necessarily what we want to be when we grow up. I can't imagine what Daddy would say if I wanted to be an artist. Suffice it to say, it wouldn't go over well.

Today, I want to be a professional writer.

I qualify "professional" because I want to be paid for it.

Technically I'm a writer already, you know, because I write. My journals, my poems, my monthly-ish movie reviews for the *Newport News*. Sometimes I can't believe I've been published since I was eleven years old. Foreshadowing, perhaps?

I'm still not sure why I was invited to this soirée. There's a chance I'm overthinking it.

The big question is . . .

What should I wear?

Chapter 22

I tell my parents everything.

Between the two of them.

My mom knows 95% of the things that go on in my life. Including books, boys, and everything in between.

With my dad, it's definitely less. There are lots of reasons for that, chief among them his lack of empathy for the teen girl experience and certain oblivion to American high school, all-inclusive "stuff." His ignorance is because of his unfamiliarity with the traditions in this country, because he wasn't born here. At least, that's what Mama says. I think it's because he's overprotective and will do everything he can to shield me from any potential source of danger, big or small, real or imagined. And for that reason, I keep (or try to keep) our conversation topics to school, family, and limited social stuff. I do this to protect myself, my freedom—or what freedom I have as a fifteen-year-old minor.

So when I mention to them that Alex invited me to her holiday party, I get very different reactions.

"I'm glad Alex invited you, it sounds like it's a good thing," Mama says.

"I can't believe you want to go after the way she treated you," Daddy counters. "You're being really stupid."

To be fair, Daddy doesn't know the whole story. I also know he doesn't really mean it, calling me stupid. I can reconcile my need for approval and my need for inclusion, though with great difficulty. Obviously, being called stupid by someone I care about doesn't feel good. It's all but soul-crushing, especially coming from a person with whom I share DNA as well as a short-fused temper.

I definitely cry about it later, after exhausting myself of tears. So much for my temper.

We don't really see my temper fuse in my household, you know, because of the good girl thing. Now that I think about it, we don't really see it anywhere except in my own psyche. That'll be interesting to see how all that suppression manifests later on.

The three of us proceed to have . . . I don't even know if you could even call it a conversation . . . about what it means if I go, and if I should go at all.

It's more like Mama and Daddy exchanging bids about what's best for me in their own cocoon of parenting principles. I'm the audience encased behind soundproof glass, witnessing and hearing everything but not actually included in a meaningful way.

At times like these, despite my consummate need to be a part of everything that has to do with me—after all, it IS my life—I know better than to interfere with their dialogue.

One time, when I was really little, I talked back to my dad. It was about something really minor, inconsequential, at least to me. I don't even remember what it was about, that's how insignificant the topic was. But it was memorable enough to engrain the message: Don't talk back to your dad.

That directive might as well be tattooed on my bicep.

So, I maintain my silence. While the three of us are sitting in our default locations around the living room—Daddy in his corner on the sofa, Mama on the well-cushioned swivel chair, and me on the opposite couch—I feel time slip by at the most glacial of paces.

Oh true apothecary! Thy drugs are not so quick. (Shakespeare again. I can't help myself.)

As ever, resolutions in this house never make port at the first go-around. I've learned this over my brief existence; that all grievances need to make air in round one. Only then can a recess take place and offline deliberations commence. Meaning, there's some more chit-chat that I, as the child, don't get to witness, the closed session. This usually takes place after bedtime when the likelihood of an interruption/eavesdropping is at its lowest.

The next day, in the morning, over his tea and toast, without so much as a greeting, Daddy says to me, "You can go to the party."

End of discussion.

I give him a hug, the bear hug kind that is a staple in our relationship.

No words are necessary, not even a thank you.

It's part of our undefinable bond. The daddy/daughter kind.

Mama just smiles at me when she comes down the stairs about an hour later. We don't need words either. The first mention of it she makes to me is, "What are you going to wear?"

She knows me so well.

Chapter 23

I don't ask Ryan to come to the party with me. After all, the invite was addressed to me only, and I don't want to be rude and inconsiderately up Alex's headcount.

This is what I tell myself.

Ryan doesn't seem to mind.

"You have a good time, hunny, it will be good for you to hang out with your friends."

For some reason his comment rubs me the wrong way, like he's the patriarch of my party participation.

Someone has control issues.

Maybe he feels left out. If that's the case, *speak up bro, I can't read your mind.*

Maybe he wants to feel like his approval matters. If that's the case, *newsflash, it doesn't.*

Maybe, just maybe, he actually wants me to have a good time hanging out with people who may or may not still technically be my "friends." If that's the case, *yikes I feel like an ass.*

I suspect it's some combination of the three.

I choose to wear dark denim skinny jeans from LOFT and a white, slightly oversized sweater, since we'll be outside most of the time, watching the boats.

At least, that's what I anticipate.

My knee-high tan boots pair well with this wintery wardrobe choice, and complement my red, cinched-at-the-waist jacket from Ralph Lauren. That Ralph knows how to craft a flattering overcoat.

As I'm brushing my now-past-my-boob-length hair, I realize I will have to go to this party alone, unarmored, and without the benefit of a bodyguard.

I feel a ball of anxiety curl in the pit of my stomach.

I realize I'm not breathing and make a half-assed attempt at sucking in some air, so my lungs can perform at an at least mediocre capacity.

The things that stress me out.

One time, I went to a yoga retreat thing at Marina Park on a Saturday by myself. I almost ran away.

Quite literally. I almost converted my mat into a magic carpet and changed direction. Thankfully, it turns out, someone greeted me before my brain cells computed the flight response. She absorbed me into their circle of wellness practitioners, and on the day went without further incidence.

This might be a *little* different. I guess I mostly just don't want to feel like I'm hovering on the periphery of some exclusive event I was only invited to as a courtesy peace offering that might not even be a peace offering, but an act of flex, an *I invited you because I could and for no other reason.*

This is where my mind goes before it's interrupted by the bing of my hair straightener, indicating it has reached max temperature and is ready to flatten my long, slightly curled hair.

I've always worn my hair long, except for that one time in seventh grade when I went to Supercuts and the guy chopped off everything to my shoulders. I have a roundish face so I pulled it off, but I didn't like it. AT ALL.

One kid, Eli Koop, announced to fifth period English, "Samantha Selim, your hair looks perfect!" across the room with cupped hands around his mouth to direct the sound path. I remember that because it made me feel better about the result.

But I've also resolved to never cut my hair more than two inches at a time ever again.

The things you learn.

I only wear buns and ponytails for physical activity. I like my hair down better. It's got this delicate curl to it, not ringlets, but a subtle sense of body that allows it to spiral by way of a diffuser or succumb to the hot plates of a straightening iron.

Charlie introduced me to hair straightening in eighth grade. I'll always be grateful for that eye-opening experience.

Before that, I barely ever even blow dried my hair.

The benefits of girlfriends, to teach you such things.

After I satisfy myself with a smear of mascara and bout of blush, I agree with my reflection staring back at me in my full-length mirror.

I text Ryan a short and sweet message of good night, hoping he takes the hint and won't text me later. I don't need to be stroking his ego while I'm out. Unless, of course, I need to pretend to be busy, should I be left on the outskirts of the gathering.

Mama drops me off at the front gate just over the bridge on the left hand side of the island. There's a bit of traffic given it's the Saturday night of the parade, which tends to be the busiest for obvious reasons. The single entry point to the island doesn't help bottlenecking matters much, either.

"Have fun hun," she says. "You can always call me if you want to come home early."

She always knows what to say to make me feel better.

Purse in hand and gameface on, I open the car door to the possibility of a good time.

I couldn't have planned what happened that night, even if I wanted to.

Chapter 24

The Norman family knows how to execute the definition of festive.

I've never seen so many twinkle lights on one building (and the Balboa Bay Club is just on the other side of the channel). Tiny bulbs ensconce every surface of the property, from the driveway to the dock. By day the house is a bright white, like snow bathed in sunlight, accented by black aluminum windows and trim. But tonight, the twinkle lights take center stage, taking advantage of the vacant canvas.

When I step out of the car, I slightly roll my right ankle so the outside of my foot meets the cement at an unnatural angle. The car door shakes a little as I struggle to catch my balance.

Great start to the night.

I wince, squeezing my eyes closed in reaction to the tight tinge of pain creeping up my leg. Mama doesn't see.

But Taylor does.

Taylor is a boy—sometimes those unisex names (Rory, Kai, Emerson, etc.) can throw you—who goes to our rival high school.

We—me and the FGP—met them during the Battle of the Bay, the football version, last year. By them, I mean Taylor, Robbie, Carmen, and Clay.

It was halftime, and we were milling about the snack stand. Nachos or hot dogs? Every teenager's concessions dilemma.

I think it was Robbie who approached us first, making some pithy remark about the quality of the meat in the hot dogs and recommending a plant-based alternative.

Apparently, that was enough to woo a gaggle of girls, famished for food, not to mention a little male attention. My friends and I were somewhat late bloomers in the boy department. We were never as flirtatious (or *loose,* as Mama might say) as some of the other girls in our class. Perhaps it was a matter of priority. We're all into school, we all want good jobs. I get that not every woman wants that. I guess that's one of the reasons we became friends in the first place. Common interest. But we obviously still have hormones and express said interest in the opposite sex.

At the time, Ryan and I had just started talking; when it rains it pours. It was nice to have some spotlight. Most of the attention I get even today is because of my bigger-than-average boobs. I started wearing a bra in third grade. I was teased endlessly by both boys and girls.

I didn't spend a lot of time with the Cove boys, since, you know, I had my own boy. But they were fun and nice, and good practice.

"You haven't even got outta the car yet and you're committing a party foul? C'mon, Selim!" Taylor chides as he helps me out of the car.

Mama's smiling as I close the door behind me.

"At least I know how to make an entrance." My quip meets Taylor's jibe, evoking a glib smile across his cheeky face. His right arm wraps around my shoulders in a half-hug on account of his tall build. I've always been vertically challenged, even with lift in my shoes, and quite frankly, I've never minded it.

I nearly forfeit my fears related to arriving at this soirée stag. Nearly. Though it doesn't show visibly on my face (I don't think), little anxieties hang like bats in a blacked-out cavern; the tiniest disturbance elicits shrieks and shouts that echo until the hollowed space regains control.

I am in control. I walk with Taylor into the foyer that extends into the main floor. An open concept, you can see the general outlines of the boats participating in the parade through floor-to-ceiling windows across the living room, which opens up to the harbor. The interior of the home feels like a winter cabin, an irony considering the beachy locale it resides within. One of the unique things about Newport is how you can see the mountains AND beach from various vantage points across the city. Who knew such a paradise could exist?

We make small talk. Taylor asks me how I've been, how Ryan is. He steers me towards the maplewood bar towards the back corner of the room. The counter is covered in every type of libation known to high school kind, accented by exactly three bowls of different flavored popcorn: butter, cheddar, and caramel delight. A shining example of our sophisticated palette.

"Are you two breaking up any time soon?" Taylor comments as he pours me a solo cup of Jingle Juice.

I think he's kidding?

Before I can answer, some guy I don't know approaches the bar area. He's tall, tan, and the quintessential surfer bro.

I'm in trouble.

"Whaddup, bro?" The unknown commodity greets Taylor with a fist bump.

"Not much man, just hanging out. You just get here?"

"Yeah, I was on a dude's boat and he just dropped me off on the dock. Promised Alex I'd roll through. Who's this?"

It takes me a few seconds before my brain registers the "this" he's referring to is yours truly. I can't tell if he's put off by the fact that it took me a minute to acknowledge his acknowledgement, if you could even call it that.

"This is Sammy Selim, from Balboa Bay," Taylor announces. "Sammy, this is Cameron Kona."

Cameron Kona. Almost but not quite alliterative. His eyes are almost as green as mine. I notice I'm noticing how much we have in common. The tellings of the tell-tale heart. Thanks for that, Mr. Poe.

"Hi," I squeak as I extend my hand towards his. He takes it delicately. His hands are soft and brown, like a well-worn baseball mit.

"Hi." His gaze meets mine in one of those perfect moments of stillness, that no one else can see except for those locked in lucidity. "You're a sophomore, too?"

"Guilty as charged."

Cameron stifles a laugh. Taylor shifts his weight between his size eleven feet uncomfortably.

"Nice, me too. What do you think of the party?"

"Well," I muse, averting my eyes towards the crowded room, trying to think of something clever to say. I spot familiar boys caught in the middle of a game of Rage Cage, chants of *"chug, chug, chug"* reverberating under the Venetian glass chandelier. "Unless these guys can grow a second stomach, I think that it's going to be a really long night for Robbie and Clay."

Cameron laughs, gently and with purpose. He takes a swig of his Bud Light before casting a sideways glance in Taylor's direction. Boys think they're so subtle, but most of the time they are as obvious as a red wine stain on white carpet.

Then, Taylor walks away. No excuse, no parting words. He just. Leaves.

Boys are weird.

And so we're alone, Cameron and I, in a sea of thirsty thrashing teens making a good time for themselves. We're in one of those underwater cages where you can see everything, but you're not actually participating in the environment. You're an observer, a bystander, a witness to life unfolding.

I don't feel like a bystander. I am very much participating, not in the party, but in this . . . whatever it is. With Cameron.

Our conversation becomes banter, which becomes teasing, which becomes touching. A poke here, a jab there. At one point his hand hangs on my arms for but a second longer than might be considered friendly, borderline flirty.

We're definitely flirting, toeing the line between friendly and flirty.

"Hey, have you seen their boat?" Cameron points to the Duffy parked slightly off to the right of the property. Duffys are these electric boats about 30 feet long. They're super easy to drive and seat up to ten people. The quintessential party boat. They were invented by a Newport local named Duffield.

We celebrated many a birthday on Alex's Duffy.

"Once or twice," I answer as casually as I can, doing my best to muffle the hint of angst in my voice.

"Let's make it three."

Cameron ignores my raspy reply, lifts my hand from the abalone-accented countertop, and pulls me, like a magnet, towards the side entrance. I didn't even know they had a side entrance.

"My mom does their interior decorating," he coaxes as he reads my facial expression like a cartographer reads his own map.

We weave our way through the crowd of faces—some drunk, some laughing, some sad. The holidays can do that to people. I haven't even seen Alex yet.

Then, as if by mind-reading magic, she appears, dressed in a long black number, looking statuesque and happy. I can't tell if it's because of the Jingle Juice or if she's actually having a good time. Maybe it's a little bit of both.

I go in for a hug and whisper-shout "Great party!" into her ear.

"Did you try the wontons?" Apparently I missed the memo on the Around the World theme. The tri-flavored popcorn threw me off.

Before she can listen to my reply, a shattering sound rings through the air already thick with the melodies of *holiday cheer*.

She scurries up the stairs faster than a deer chasing a rabbit, and that's saying a lot given the five-inch heels she's wearing.

We take that as a cue to resume our mission. There are a few people, mostly couples, scattered along the beltway, like call boxes on the highway, evenly spaced and tied up in their own world. My highway to the danger zone.

Cameron steps first onto the boat, a modern day act of chivalry. I follow him. At the far end of the boat is a cozy corner padded with pillows and throw blankets made of sherpa. He sits, creating just enough space for me between his arm and where the seating begins.

So, I sit. I'm not nervous or anxious. I'm all kinds of calm, actually. I'm enjoying myself.

Cameron smells like pot and mint. He makes for a nice headrest.

The house glows from within and without. Laughter bounces through the channel and reverberates to create its own holiday hymn. Boat horns add to this symphony of sorts. But all I hear is Cameron.

We talk a little more. Nothing happens besides this, whatever this is. He doesn't try to kiss me, which is a blessing for obvious reasons, but also kind of insulting.

Eventually, someone sees us and starts howling at us to get out of the boat. Something about it being dangerous.

We walk up to the house and rejoin the festivities. Taylor swoops in and tags Cameron into a game of beer pong. The two of them play for a while, trading shots and words. I watch for a bit, hanging back so as not to crowd, but close enough to study Cameron's face. It's different in the light. It's golden and soft, freckles sprinkled sparingly across his cheeks. I blink a lot so it doesn't look like I'm staring.

I see it then, his face changing. It goes from glittering and floating, to dejected and annoyed. His green eyes turn black.

That could only mean one thing.

Chapter 25

"I thought you knew I had a boyfriend."

It sounds so absurd when I say it, but in saying it, I almost believe it to be true. My thoughts swim between *I'm sure Taylor or someone must've told him* and *I'm not sure if boys talk about these things.*

Cameron doesn't say much after the big reveal. Why would he? I wish he would. It would make me feel like less of a liar by omission. That sounds selfish.

The noise of my thoughts drown out the fun of the night. In my own bevvy of bristled hope, I'm not happy anymore. I guess I was earlier. Happy, consumed by the rushing sensation of anticipation, teetering on the edge of possibility. I've fallen off the cliffs of dare and onto the rocks of despair.

The rocks are sharp and angled, piercing. They poke holes in my soul. Dramatic.

In an ideal world, I want Cameron to be okay with my unavailability and want to spend time with me, despite my off-the-market status. Can't boys and girls be friends without the subtext of disloyalty to a partner? By the looks of things, this boy's behaviors betray his thoughts.

My own behaviors probably do too. I'm just not ready to admit it.

Not yet.

When I get home, a lingering energy makes it difficult for me to fall asleep. Excitement. Sadness. Like blowing air into a balloon, then immediately letting it out. Maybe Cameron and I can be friends? Maybe he'll realize how much he enjoyed spending time with me, and want to hang out anyway?

In the back of my mind, in the part of my consciousness I refuse to acknowledge, I know it's not likely. I know it's not fair.

But I'll dream about tonight anyways. Because that's probably the way only I can remember it, relive it. Because my dreams belong to me, even if this boy doesn't.

Chapter 26

Belonging is a complicated concept. There is material possession; belonging to someone, like a boyfriend; or something belonging to you, like a piece of jewelry. There is the sense of belonging, of being a part of or included in the greater whole—such as in a family, a community.

The first definition of belonging that comes up in my Google search is an affinity for a place or situation. Belongingness, according to Wikipedia, is the human emotional need to be an accepted member of a group. Whether it is family, friends, co-workers, a religion, or something else, people tend to have an 'inherent' desire to belong and be an important part of something greater than themselves.

Humans are emotional creatures. I'd argue teen girls bear the brunt of the extremes of these feelings. I speak from personal experience. I'm living it.

Chapter 27

My mom has a big family. A really big family. I have about twenty cousins, all from her side. Mom is the oldest of six, and the only girl at that. Age wise, I fall in the middle of the pack. The oldest cousin is about ten years older than me, and she has a kid. (I consider her a cousin, too.) One of my aunts is pregnant. The group is still growing.

My uncle Gordon usually hosts the annual Christmas gathering. He lives pretty close by, in Mission Viejo. Because we have such a large family, we always do a Secret Santa exchange—one for the cousins and one for the adults. And a potluck.

Last year, I had to wear a turtleneck because SOMEONE left a surprise (or seven) on my neck. I pretended to be mad (I was more irritated than anything) but I felt kinship with Rizzo and her "hickey from Kenickie." A cinematic bond spanning space, time, and hairstyles. My cousin Tiffany thought it was cool. My sister Jenny just made fun of me.

That was early on in our relationship, the honeymood period. When Ryan curated Spotify playlists for me on the regular. When he would show up at the end of my yoga class and take me for ice cream at Salt & Straw.

At this year's Christmas gathering, when Tiffany asks me about Ryan, I just say, "He's good, busy being a college guy." Because I'm dating a college guy.

She thinks it's cool.

<h1 style="text-align:center">Chapter 28</h1>

Over winter break, Ryan lets me drive his pick-up truck.

He didn't have to, but he does.

I have my learner's permit. And finished one of the three driver's ed classes you're required to take before applying for an official license. I'm nearly an expert.

I can tell he's nervous. But seriously? We're in a parking lot.

Ryan never asked me about the boat parade party. He didn't even call me that night. While, yes, we said good night *before* the party, most times that doesn't stop him.

So I bring it up.

"Alex's party was fun," I chime after a tight left turn into the Quail Street corporate plaza.

"Oh yeah? I'm so glad, are you friends again?"

Okay, he must be distracted.

"Babe, it will take more than one invite to a party to rectify all this business we're dealing with." I take one hand off the wheel to emphasize the scope of the issue by waving my hand in circular motions. He cringes in the passenger seat.

"I didn't even see her most of the night . . . "

Whoops.

"Oh? Who'd you hang out with?"

Normally, I would be offended by that question. But I'm too caught up in my own story to notice.

Cooly, the words, "Some people from Newport Cove, you know, from my yoga class," escape my lips. I leave it at that.

"Oh nice."

Good job Sam, he doesn't suspect a thing.

Not that there's anything to suspect. I didn't do anything wrong. Right?

Let's go through the night. There was some flirting. There was some touching, but nothing boundary crossing. To be honest I'm surprised Ryan hasn't mentioned our own sex life, or more accurately, lack thereof.

For the record, I'm still not ready and not interested in making *that* a part of our relationship. I know he feels differently. It's weird he hasn't mentioned it lately.

But it works for me. So I don't question it.

I think part of the reason is because he wants it so much, that it's almost like, well, what if you don't get it? How will that make our relationship different? *Would* our relationship be different? At this point, I'm not sure I want to find out. Because I have a feeling it would be a bad-different. As in, that's all he'd want to do, different.

It's probably my fears talking. But they're real and earnest. We haven't addressed these reasons yet. It's partly my fault for not sharing them. And partly his for not trying to understand the reasons.

Feigning compliance doesn't count. That's status quo, and status quo is the opposite of action. It's inaction. We should be moving forward, and that is on both of us.

It's almost dinner time and I need to get home.

"What do you say to me driving home?"

"Fat chance," he gawks as he leans over the center console to kiss me.

He tastes sweet and tart. Like sugar mixed with salt.

Sometimes it's hard to tell the difference between the two. But salt makes the sugar sweeter.

Chapter 29

College is coming. Daddy suggested I visit some campuses over the next few years, to get a sense of what it's like to be there, amongst the buildings and students. It's decided Mama and I will take a trip this winter break to see some of the California schools.

There are so many schools in this country, it's insane. I won this book (from scoring the highest on an SAT practice test, no less) by the Princeton Review that basically summarizes facts and figures about 357 colleges and universities in the US. How is a kid supposed to choose from so many options? Granted, we all have different interests and qualifications. I know there are kids whose parents are *obsessed* with their kids going to a top-tier school—whatever that means. My dad happens to be one of them. At least, it comes off that way. Sometimes I think he gets so into the hype of it all that it consumes his every thought. We're alike in that way. When we commit to something, we commit—sometimes to the extreme. He's only human. I forget that sometimes. Just because parents are adults doesn't mean they have all the answers.

But then he says things like, "I just want you to get a good education, so you can get a good job, and take care of yourself." It's very un-Indian of him, at least for his generation when it comes to daughters. He's always wanted the best for us, all three of his kids. He wants us to grow up American. That's why, he says, he never tried to teach us Urdu when we were little kids, when language acquisition was easiest. Some vocabulary, yes, but not the *language*. He says it would be too confusing for us to separate the two. I don't know what "two" he's referring to: Urdu and English, or our identities as Indian-Americans. Honestly, it's probably both.

I get where he's coming from. It's a little confusing. But I think it's confusing because it feels like there's a part of us he's hiding, to protect us. But from what? From ourselves? I think he's protecting us from his own experiences, as an immigrant, as a stranger. He doesn't want us to be strangers in our home. I get that. But someday, I will decide for myself. And we'll go from there.

Today, though, I follow the rules of the house.

There's a bookcase in our house that's entirely devoted to textbooks. Not our school textbooks; textbooks Daddy orders directly from the publishers. They're different from the ones we use in school, as their primary role is to give us extra practice. They're mostly math, some science, some reading. Every Saturday morning, Daddy assigns us "problems" to do. They take about two hours to complete. Right now it's Jenny and me; Andrew is still a bit young. Mama helps us with all the history and writing stuff. The division of responsibility is somewhat stereotypical, but it works.

We're always about two years ahead of the school curriculum. I'm working on Calculus now.

"It never hurts to be the best." An infamous Ashar-ism.

Mama and I leave on our California College Tour the Sunday after Christmas. We figure we'll be gone four or five days—we haven't really decided yet. She's more of the go-with-the-flow type.

Our plan so far is to get to Solvang/Buellton tonight, and then Carmel for night two.

Jenny and Andrew aren't used to being alone with Daddy. It's always the five of us at home. And Mama really took care of us for the most part when we were little. We'll see how that goes.

We stop to visit Ryan at Lululemon on our way out. It's honestly kind of out of the way, but Mama was sweet to insist we say hi before we take off for a few days. Funny that Mama is the first to suggest it, and not me. Hmm.

Ryan started working at Lululemon a few days a week for extra cash. I'm kind of jealous that he has a big boy job. I think I'd be good at retail. All my time is spent poring over textbooks and practice tests. I know that's not entirely true, but compared to my other classmates and influencers on social, it feels that way.

He even gets a discount! Those yoga pants aren't cheap. Good quality, yes. And I like the designs they have. My favorite are the pink and white peony ones.

Ryan's with a customer when I walk in. I meander to the sales rack and pick up a white sports bra that would never fit me. Sports bras were invented in 1975. It's really not that long ago. I wonder what women's exercise clothing options were before then? I should look it up.

"Can I help you find something, Miss?" His winning smile greets me first, followed by a peck on the lips.

"Are you always so intimate with your customers?" I slide my arms around his waist for a quick squeeze.

"Only the ones who are my girlfriend." Good answer. "Are you ready for your trip?"

"Yeah, it will be nice to spend some time with Mama. And see the schools. It'll be nice to actually experience what I've been working for, in some sense . . . if that makes sense."

"The most sensical." He's mocking me. I like it when he mocks me. It shows he's listening.

"Mama's waiting, so I should go. See you next week." I stand on my tippy toes to kiss his cheek. I don't really need to stand on my tippy toes, but it feels romantic somehow, like a knee pop from a 1950s movie.

"See you. Love you, babe."

I'm already out the door when he says this last part. I pretend not to hear and keep walking.

The drive is scenic, up through LA and past the sprawl of Ventura. We pass Rincon, a surf spot Ryan told me about once. His dad taught him to surf here. It's a point break, where the wave breaks on both sides of the peak, like at 18th Street at home. It's cool to put a (wave) face to a name.

I understand now why UCSB has so much appeal. In addition to the surf spot outside Goleta, Isla Vista is a happening neighborhood.

I've heard stories about Halloween here, which supposedly lasts all weekend, and the legacy of Floatopia—where a bunch of drunk kids take inner tubes, rafts, and unicorns into the waves and hang out behind the break. This is what we call a party school. I won't go to a party school, but it's cool to see what it entails. And let's face it, all schools have parties. Reputations are heresy. It's the truth that's personal.

The truth is, I want to go to a school with a football team. It sounds counterintuitive, seeing as I am not an athlete and mostly focused on academics. I want to go to a school with identity, with gusto and spirit. Where being a student alone means instant induction into the family. I realize most schools are like that too, but football, that's an event. That's a pastime.

It's not really about the football team. Most schools with football teams have name recognition. Good school, good job. That's the formula. Or so I've been told.

UCSB doesn't have a football team.

But it sure is beautiful.

We get to Solvang when it's really, really dark. And it's only 6 p.m. Solvang is about forty miles from Santa Barbara, depending on what road you take. The drive is about an hour. The winter solstice just passed, and the days are starting to get longer again. But the nights still take up a majority of the twenty-four-hour cycle.

Solvang is like a mini Copenhagen transplanted to sunny Southern California. (Though as we go north, it's not as sunny as often. You know, as we get further away from the equator.) It's got the cutest bakeries and restaurants, and also lots of wineries. Mama will buy some wine for herself. I feel bad for cramping her style. She likes to go out, though she rarely does, being home with us kids. I heard stories about her 50th birthday, which is also when she got her first cell phone. Generational differences! I'll be 21 in just over five years. We'll indulge together then.

There's a statue of the Little Mermaid, like the one in Copenhagen. And a park dedicated to Hans Christian Andersen. The Mission Santa Ynez is down the street, too. We studied the missions and the El Camino Real in fourth grade. We each got assigned a mission. Mine was San Luis Rey, just inland of Oceanside. I was lucky; we got to visit because it was within driving distance. I've always liked old buildings. They're built to last (unlike the cheap stuff we make today. Capitalism at its finest). If those walls could talk.

We're tired, so we get take out—sausages, obviously—and turn in early.

Breakfast at Brekkie is amazing. We follow it up with pastries for dessert. When in Denmark. There's something poetic about eating danish pastries in a Danish town.

"What kind do you want?" Mom asks.

"Um." I'm not sure how to word my response. "Can we get a bunch of different ones, you know, so we can try different flavors?"

She smiles at me, like only a mother who sees herself in her daughter can.

"Exactly what I was thinking. There's nothing wrong with leftovers."

This is why we're soulmates.

We continue along the coast, driving up the 101. I think about that Phantom Planet song. On through wine country, Santa Maria, a drive-by of SLO, Atascadero, King City, Salinas—the hometown of John Steinbeck. Much of his work takes place in this region. It screams *East of Eden*. Mama is excited about this part. Although, this part of the state all looks the same to me: fields. Lots and lots of fields. I suspect this area inspired the line *amber waves of grain* from "America the Beautiful."

Keeping with the plan, we decide to stay in Carmel, or Carmel-by-the-Sea, as it's officially named. We backtrack a bit since it's southwest of Salinas. Definitely worth it.

This town reminds me of something I think would exist on a Spanish island. The architecture has this mission revival theme going on, mixed with a more coastal cottage vibe. The famed Pebble Beach golf course rests down the peninsula overlooking Carmel Bay.

We get here by 3 p.m. or so, with still enough light left to explore. The boutiques channel a warm, artsy bazaar feel, reminiscent of Laguna Beach. Lots of paintings, photography, jewelry. I am a sucker for artisanal jewelry. The handiwork, the eye of the artist, how the synchronicity of both skills creates beauty incarnate.

When I was ten, I won a black pearl as a prize for second place in a writing contest at our local library. Obviously Mama suggested I enter. She's solely responsible for me discovering my love of writing.

At first, not gonna lie, I wasn't too hot on winning a black pearl. What's a ten-year-old supposed to do with a black pearl?

"When you're older," Mama would say, "maybe you can make a piece of jewelry out of it. It will be a symbol of how much you love writing, and how it's always been a part of your life."

That got me excited. What would I make? A necklace? A bracelet? A ring? What metals would I use? (Lately I've been into rose gold. It's a brighter, more luminescent version of copper.) Whenever I visit jewelry vendors in their kiosks full of wearable art, I always think of what I'll make. When? Who knows. That's part of the intrigue. I'll know it when it's time.

Today, I buy a matching bracelet and necklace, entirely made of steel masquerading as silver, and black stone. Connecting the black stones with a piece of black leather, the bracelet hangs tight on my wrist. I have really small wrists. I can wrap my hand around it so that my thumb and index finger touch without any issue. Mama and Jenny have bigger bones. Funny how even in one family your shape can vary. Genes are fascinating.

The necklace, less intricate, showcases a matching single black stone like a pendant, and ties around my neck by two black cords, accented by silver beads at the ends. No one will see them, because my hair hides the place where they meet, but I like knowing they're there. It's like a secret only we know about.

Mama finds a necklace with a silver pendant in the shape of a heart, also with a black cord that wraps around the nape of her neck. We're matching, kind of. We do that a lot. Sometimes on purpose, sometimes on accident.

Sometimes our closeness breeds resentment.

We decide to have dinner at a cute little bistro a few buildings over from our hotel. Reminiscent of an Italian sidewalk cafe, each table dons a red and white checkered tablecloth topped off by a single tea light. Simple, yet chic.

Right in the middle of our sausage and pepper pizza, Jenny calls. It's about seven o'clock, which is late for dinner in our household. But when we're away, we do as the time suits.

"Hi hun," Mama greets Jenny after she pulls her phone from the outside pocket of her black purse backpack. "We're just having pizza for dinner."

I think she's going to say she'll call her back after we eat.

But she doesn't.

Instead, I hear a one-sided exchange of, "We went to Solvang yesterday, ate some pastries, now we're in Carmel, you'd like it here, it reminds me a lot of Laguna . . ."

Can you call her back later, I beg with my eyes, *while we're not in the middle of dinner? I hardly ever get to be alone with you for a meal, she's just trying to ruin our evening . . .*

Then Andrew gets on the phone.

I'm not proud of this, but I lose it.

"Mommmm! Can we finish eating? You can talk to them later!"

I don't get it. I would *never* take a call in the middle of dinner, unless it was a real emergency. I don't even text during dinner. Am I a total anomaly?

"Hold on, Sam, I'm just talking to your brother."

She speaks so calmly, like she's not doing anything wrong.

Her calmness stokes my anger.

"So it's more important to talk to Andrew than it is to talk to me?"

I don't feel irrational as I say this. Because in this moment, I believe I am making a valid point. *I'm sitting right in front of you, I think, and you're choosing to talk to my siblings who are bored at home, and you're entertaining their boredom. While I am sitting here staring at a pizza with nothing else to do but wait for you to get off the phone.*

My insides get hot and my face escalates in temperature. Why am I getting so worked up? Because I always end up in this situation. I'm the oldest, so I can wait. I'm the oldest, so I can spare a few minutes because Jenny and Andrew need some extra attention. I'm the oldest, so I have responsibilities, duties that come with the territory.

Birth order theory has its merits. I'm the first to admit I model the traits of the first born: achiever, likes to be right about stuff, strives to please others, reliable, helpful, protective. I don't get as much attention anymore as when I did when I was younger. I'm okay with that, for the most part. I know my parents love us all equally, but sometimes they treat us differently, because, well, we are different. Neither of them would overtly choose to favor one or the other. But that doesn't mean it doesn't happen, on accident or without them realizing it. That's the part that's hardest to deal with.

There are moments like these when I just want to spend time with my mom, uninterrupted and alone with each other. Maybe I'll never have it like I want it. Maybe it's an ideal I'll never have in reality. Maybe I need to accept that, and move on.

But I'm still angry, a mix of sad and helpless. Because I can't control it. But I can control how I react.

Now I feel bad.

I just went through ten different emotions in ten minutes. It's pretty normal, though. Hormones often take my heart hostage.

By the time Mama hangs up the phone, I'm crying, sucking in deep breaths, trying to hide the pain from my belly. Better to let it out than keep it in.

Between sobs, I try to explain the narrative that just played out in my head. I figure she was the oldest in her family, too, so maybe she'll get it.

"I'm sorry you're upset. But you don't have to be. I'm right here."

She doesn't get it. Maybe she did, one day, when she was a teenager fighting for her mom's attention amongst a brethren of boys. Maybe she's forgotten, because she's had a lifetime of perspective. I won't ever know for sure. Either way, just because our parents are parents, doesn't mean they have all the answers.

I whine a little more, maybe another five minutes or so, then move on. I've made my point to myself, as clear as I know how to make it. Sometimes even those we love just don't understand. That hurts like nothing else. That's why I'm learning to love myself.

I saw a meme on Instagram with a quote (attributed to) Bob Marley. Who knows if he actually said it—can't trust the web at all these days, but the spirit of the words strikes me every time I think about them. In fact, I wrote them in my journal. That's how you know they made an impact on me.

It says:

"Truth is everybody is going to hurt you: you just gotta find the ones worth suffering for."

This goes for parents, too. They'll hurt you, even when they don't mean to. Divorce. There's an example. They're flesh and bone, too. Equally fragile. More experienced, yes. But also, people making their own way through the world on their own journeys. I haven't really thought about that; not in this way, at least. There's something to it, though. I will noodle on it.

After hugs and kisses, I fall asleep next to Mama. I'm exhausted from the driving, from the walking, from the iron my heart pumped over dinner and after. I deep sleep tonight. I'm not usually a deep sleeper. I usually hover around the first phase of sleep throughout the night, although biologically that's probably impossible. My brain never fully turns off into the tabula rosa state some people describe.

The next day, after a quick stop at a local café, we continue on PCH towards San Francisco. PCH basically runs the length of the coast. Yes, we've seen one school so far, technically. But we'll hit a few more today.

We literally cruise through Santa Cruz for about an hour. I've heard this area described as a hippy surf town.

They're not wrong. While not necessarily my cup of darjeeling tea, it's definitely charming in its own way. We drive up the mountain (really big hill?) towards UC Santa Cruz.

There is a lot of green.

We end up amongst some cabin-like structures that might be dorms or some kind of student housing.

There is even more green.

The trees climb towards the sun, which you can't really see since the needles create a patchwork canopy that nearly blocks it from view. It's dark for noon. Going to college here must be like camping 24/7.

I love nature, but camping isn't really my scene. The Selim family version of camping involves a fifty-two-foot motorhome.

My dad planned a couple of these trips for us when we were little—to Yosemite one year, and Yellowstone the next. That was almost ten years ago. I think I'd enjoy it now, too. I prefer that to the train when it comes to mode of transportation. In either case, I don't know how else you could see SO much of these united, mostly contiguous and utterly contrastive states.

I probably won't go here. There's no football team. But I'm glad we've seen it. It's nice to know it exists.

Continuing northward, we hit SF around four in the afternoon. It's hazy, misty even. I hear every neighborhood has its own climate. I've never seen so many (what I think are) homes/apartments/condos/skyscrapers so close together on so many hills. I also hear it's legal to be naked in SF.

We stayed at Candlestick Park on the way up to Yosemite during that RV trip. During that visit we did the touristy things, like ride a cable car, eat hot pot in Chinatown, enjoy a scenic view of the Golden Gate Bridge (though I'm sure locals do those things, too). Today, we're taking in a different perspective: that of a future college kid. So we drive by SFSU, UCSF (though that's a graduate school only, I think) and see the bridge again, because how can we not.

We traipse over the Bay Bridge towards Berkeley so we can see Cal. It's on the same side of the bay as Oakland. Different from SF. This side of the bay seems misunderstood. It's got its own identity—each neighborhood does, like SF. I hear it's sunnier over here, too.

Magnificently large wrought iron gates guard one of the entrances to Cal's campus. Like a boundary between student life and real life. We take a photo here, on the boundary, on the line between what's real and what's to come. Who knows if it's here I'll even be? But I like the symbolism.

What I'm really excited about is chucking our U-y and heading south again towards Palo Alto, home to Stanford University. All I know so far about Stanford: it's the Ivy of the West Coast.

The more we drive around the area, the more I feel the tech bubble floating around us. There are buildings with company names I've never heard of, next to buildings like Tesla. We drive through Sand Hill Road because I'm curious what "big tech" looks like.

It's clean. It's neutral. All I'm seeing are the buildings, though. Does the inside reflect the outside? One can only assume.

For the last twenty years, from the dotcom boom and onward, lots and lots of people have made their way up here searching for two things: careers and capital. It's like the show "Silicon Valley" or the movie "The Social Network." Girl has an idea, girl pitches to investors, girl gets funding, girl makes it happen. Though, aside from the Katrina Lakes and Sara Blakelys, there's not a whole lot of women. I don't see myself as a coder/programmer/developer, but that will change with my generation. It's changing already.

Stanford is . . . collegial. My words don't usually fail me, but if there was ever a space that epitomized my ideal of what a college town/campus would look like, this is it. Lots of shopping, lots of food, lots of bookstores, all with charm and sophistication at the same time.

The campus is what I'd describe as Old World California. Like the towns we've seen along the drive over the past few days. Missions and palm trees. And some red brick. Actually, lots of red bricks. It is also very clean. I sense a theme.

We wait until the morning to walk around and take it all in. It's brisk, the weather. It smells like pine; not the kind from air fresheners, but real pine, from the forest. There's no one around, really, save for the morning joggers in their headbands and sherpa zip-ups. School is out, and I like it quiet like this. I like quiet in general. You can hear the buildings, the echo from passersby, birds, and obviously squirrels. Can't forget the squirrels. (Apparently these rodents are staples across many schools in California.)

I'm legit wearing a hat and scarf to accessorize my puffy black jacket and ugg boots, it's that cold. (I will never give up my ugg boots. As with my rainbows. And my Jack's hoodie.) I have gloves too, but it's hard to take pics with them on. I need those ones that are either fingerless or work with touchscreens.

We wander through the arches—there's lots of arches. High and mighty, almost cathedral-like in presence. As far as I know, this school is non-denominational. It's a sign.

"Look at the rose garden!" Mama calls from a seemingly miles-long array of every different rose you could ever imagine. And it's *December*. That's impressive.

And there's a football stadium. College kids tailgate before games, where they grill hot dogs, play drinking games, and hang out in the parking lot. I like the term *tailgate*. It sounds so . . . collegial.

I need to work on my vocabulary. College kids are probably more eloquent than this.

Daddy calls and basically chides us to get home ASAP. Even when we're four hundred miles away, he has a magnetism.

"We'll see you tonight, then. Don't let your mom drive off a cliff." Gotta love that humor.

I don't tell him we're taking PCH back. The view is WAY better than the 101. And entirely coastal. It'll take a little longer, but it's worth it. The first leg wraps along the cliffs, in and out, like a snake making serpentine movements while hugging the mountain's face.

I start getting carsick the eighth or ninth turn in. Maybe this wasn't the best idea? I realize it's a *you've seen one, you're seen them* all kind of thing.

This too shall pass.

"Mom, look, it's Hearst Castle. It's so tiny from here."

Hearst Castle is a legit castle. Its history is one of dark and light periods, as are most histories. I've only seen pictures. Most of the spaces are dipped in gold. A little extravagant for my taste. It's fascinating to see what people spend their money on, and even more fascinating, why.

We don't stop today because we're on a schedule.

Well, we stop in front of the beach below, infamous for its elephant seal presence. In fact I think it's called Elephant Seal Vista Point.

It's a long day of driving, and we get home around eight. We stop for dinner at Del Taco. I don't know what it is about the cheeseburgers there, but it's my favorite item on the menu. Go figure.

Jenny and Andrew are happy to see us. Well, they're happy to see Mama. I'm just the big sis, remember. We all have our roles. I'm like their second mom. At our ages, it's not well received, since I'm bossy. When we're older they'll appreciate me more. Maybe.

Chapter 30

Beth Winchelle likes to blab. She's nice enough, but she's always stirring some heated, seething pot of gossipy gumbo whatever chance she gets.

The first time we met, she told me she wished she had my boobs and my butt.

Thank you?

She's on the school's dance team. It's more respected than the cheerleading squad. The dancers are very talented. Their fortes mimic the magic of a ballerina in a music box. Before I got into yoga, I danced. I still do. It's just mostly with my mom in our kitchen on weeknights. I auditioned for the team each of the last two years and didn't make it. It's highly competitive.

When Beth shares her tidbit of the day, I take it with a grain of salt.

"Sam, I have to tell you something." She's sitting behind me in our fifth period French class. Her voice buzzes behind my left ear like a mosquito looking for its next victim. Finals are coming, and Madame Schumacher is reviewing *vocabulaire alimentaire*. I always get boisson (drink) and poisson (fish) mixed up.

"What is it, Beth?" My pitch hovers slightly above what's natural, the way it does when I'm trying to be overly nice.

"Kylie just told me that Ryan was hanging out with her sister over the weekend."

My heart starts treading water.

"They were in the jacuzzi in Little Canyon."

My heart tires from the effort and loses energy.

"Alone."

My heart stops and bobs like a cork.

"She said he asked her if she'd do him if he weren't taken."

My heart floods, and finally sinks.

Kylie's sister is Lucie, part of Alex's and Charlie's circle, and I guess my former friend by affiliation. The one I tried calling about AP World before school started.

She's a water polo prodigy. She'll go to a top college program.

She dated a junior last year. Well, not really dated. He asked her to be his date to prom, because he thought she was hot. That's what I heard. I don't know anything else about it. I try not to fuel the rumor mill, but sometimes I am guilty of it.

"Oh." I manage to form at least that one sound.

"Yeah, I'm sorry. I thought you should know."

How considerate.

I want to say, *you're not sorry. I can see the pleasure in your face, the devilish snare behind your eyes.*

Instead, I go with a neutral, monotone, "Thanks."

As in, *thanks for adding yet another line item to my list of grievances re: Ryan.*

As in, *thanks for resurfacing the sex issue that is not so dormant.*

As in, *thanks for interrupting my French vocabulary review.*

Just, thanks. A. Lot.

During sixth period, Mark nudges—or rather, pokes—my shoulder from behind.

What is with people poking me today?

"What do you want?" My roar of a reply must strike Mark as odd.

"What's got your panties in a twist?" He eyes me with a genuine curiosity. "I've never seen you so . . . not nice."

I respond with silence.

"Boyfriend trouble? Lay it on me. I can help."

My forehead scrunches up, because I can't control my eyes opposing gravity.

"I doubt that."

"Try me."

"I think he was in a jacuzzi with another girl." I pause for effect. "Alone."

Mark laughs, not like he's responding to a joke, but like he's not surprised by this turn of events.

"You haven't slept with him, huh? Figures," he says before I acknowledge his comment.

My face contorts again.

He continues.

"He just wants some sexual attention, like any horny college guy. Don't be so surprised."

"I get that, really, I do. But what about me?"

Mark closes his eyes and shakes his head.

"No, Sammy, I don't think you do."

I need to confront Ryan. But how? When? It's taking all I have to restrain myself from verbally accosting my boyfriend.

Naturally, my fuse is pretty short. My mom, for comparison, has a long fuse. She seethes over a period of time before releasing her rage. I am more like my dad. However, I seem to adjust my behavior depending on my audience and/or my patience. Situationally, it will depend on which one takes favor.

I decide it's best that I wait until I see him in person, so I can read his body language and infer his tone. 93% of communication is nonverbal, after all.

I'll see him Friday night for dinner and a movie. We can be such a cliché, can't we?

Chapter 31

"We just talked, nothing happened."

"That's not why I'm mad."

"Why are you mad?"

"Because you *propositioned* another girl while neither of you had any clothes on. Not to mention, she happens to be someone I know pretty well."

"So you wouldn't be mad if it was someone you didn't know?"

This conversation is not going well. Since I found out from Beth about Ryan's hot tub outing, I can't think of anything else but him, half-naked, breathing in the same chlorine-infused steam as another girl within a ten-foot diameter.

Note to self: don't wait these things out, it only makes you crazier.

We're eating dinner at the CPK at Fashion Island, keeping with the cliché. Basic AF.

I gulp in a fresh breath before taking a sip of my Shirley Temple. He's obviously not getting it.

"No, I'd still be mad. But I wouldn't think about it every single time I passed her in the halls, which is GUESS WHAT, EVERY DAY." My voice is even until those last six syllables. (*Every* has three today, for emphasis.) Then it ascends like a concerto. "Why would you even ask her if she wanted to sleep with you, anyway? Do you know how mortifying that is for me?"

I don't mean to make it about me. But I'm really hurt. And I deserve to know.

"I dunno, babe." Ryan's voice is solemn and taught. "I guess I just wanted to know if I'm desirable."

"Are you *kidding* me?"

I'm losing it.

"Do you know how insecure you sound right now? It's not like you're some hot new product and you get to test the market to see what consumers think of you. That's not how this works."

Heads are turning in our direction. Thankfully we're in a back corner booth, so the visual of us isn't so overt. The acoustics are another story.

"How does it work, Sammy, hmm? You won't even touch me."

"That is not true. You sound like a whiny baby who doesn't like his curfew. You have no right to go around soliciting yourself like a hooker."

Ryan winces. "It's not exactly the same thing. And I was not soliciting myself. I was asking a woman a hypothetical question. I didn't do it to make you upset or angry. I just wanted to know."

He sounds so pathetic. I see tears brimming in his eyes, but don't call him out on it. I'll save that ammo for later if needed.

The sad part is, I actually believe him. I truly don't think he meant anything by it, but when we have the dynamic that we do, with the "friends" that we have, there need to be boundaries. And he totally just long-jumped over the baseline of what is fair with this little escapade.

I'll forgive him, but I won't forget.

"Why didn't you ask me?" My eyes meet his, their earnestness genuine and sincere.

The silence is deafening.

"Honestly . . ." he lengthens the *eee* a little too long. "I didn't think to ask you."

Ouch? Not sure how to feel here.

"I will next time, though."

Next time? Great. Can't wait for that.

I really don't want to see this movie anymore. Supposedly it's a rom-com about how two writers meet on a beach and end up getting married.

Who's living that story?

Chapter 32

A new semester begins. There are some shufflings of class schedules, grievances emoted around grades. My routine remains unchanged. And that includes my visits to the library.

In third period, Mr. Ishuda decides it would be cute to host something of an awards ceremony, acknowledging last semester's highlights (and some might argue, lowlights).

Guess who earns the highest grade in the class?

We have a class portal where we can log in and view our grades. There's also a field for class rank. Last time I checked, my rank had a little "1" next to it.

So in class, I'm not surprised. *Mortified* is probably the right word. Proud, yet sheepish.

Mr. Ishuda hands me the certificate, commemorating my achievement. He nods curtly, offering a brusque "Well done" while feigning the tough exterior he's known for. This is the same person that also spins as a DJ on the weekends. I don't see those two aspects being dimensions of the same person, but people surprise you.

I hear a snicker erupt from the back row.

It's Chad. Of course.

Chad is a know-it-all. When it comes to chem, it seems like he really does know it all. He's into cars and spark plugs and all that mechanical magic. He just doesn't do his homework.

I feel like an imposter, because I know he's smarter than me when it comes to molecules and moles. On the other hand, I did the work.

Daddy says he's jealous, that he's embarrassed a girl beat him in the books.

"Did you beat Chad?" Daddy enjoys the spoils of his kids' academic conquests. "Cream always comes to the top." Ah yes, another proverb.

I let it go.

"Mark, you're sitting here."

Teachers reserve the right to update their seating chart for each class period "at their discretion." Mostly intended to account for changes in students' schedules in the new semester. In my experience, there hasn't been a whole lot of movement.

Until today.

Miss Wally decides Mark will enjoy sixth period English from across the room, far and away from his original seat behind me.

Apparently we've been too disruptive so far this year.

This is a first for me. I've never been party to a seat assignment change, *ever*. At least, not in this way.

In seventh grade, all those middle school years ago, my then-Language Arts teacher Mr. Bruno thought it would be effective to seat the class troublemaker behind me. You know, to encourage him to not be so disruptive and actually behave in class, dare he even learn something.

I'm not one to stare down teachers. But for this situation I made an exception.

Mr. Bruno still teases me about that death glare, as he calls it. Wrinkled nose, laser-focused eyes, pouty lips. My face looked like a deviously angry Pillsbury DoughBoy, with tanned skinned and hazel green eyes.

Being a good student has its disadvantages. Such as, it makes you an automatic chess piece in the game of classroom decorum. Where the teacher is the queen, or king, or omnipotent ruler.

Mark laughs as he takes his new seat as indicated by Miss Wally's pointer finger.

"Something funny, Mark?"

"Not at all." A wink flits over in my direction.

I consider floating a death glare in his direction. I settle on sticking my tongue out at him. Seems more appropriate given the circumstances.

I mean, we just got broken up.

Chapter 33

My dad needs surgery. A recent check-up with his cardiologist revealed some not-so-insignificant blockage in his arteries. I saw the x-rays from the angiogram. I wasn't sure what I was looking at.

Daddy has been pretty healthy for most of his (and my) life. Aside from a freak bicycle accident where he shattered his pelvis, by way of some kid cutting him off near Main Street in Huntington Beach, he's never been in the hospital for an extended period of time. Even that incident happened before I was born. He's getting older, and so increases the likelihood of health concerns and visits to the doctor.

I hate hospitals. They're sterile and bland and too bright. They have this way of seeming empty and full at the same time. I associate hospitals with bad news. My grandma slept in the Santa Monica Hospital for four months before she passed. I was barely ten years old. My limited experience has colored my glasses from rose to a stormy gray.

"It's pretty routine, Sammy, try not to worry." My mama, ever the consoler.

What could possibly be routine about opening up someone's chest in a room flooded with stage lights, using instruments that don't make music?

This isn't a morning walk or a trip to the grocery store. Why is she so calm?

The surgery takes place on a Tuesday morning. It happens to be finals week, so we get out of school early, around lunchtime.

Marci and Victor Vepti pick us up from school. They have three daughters—one my age, one Jenny's age, and one Andrew's age. When we were younger, we were all friends with our Vepti counterparts. Time separated us, as well as different interests (boys), academic habits (or lack thereof) and general preferences for friends.

We go to Taco Bell as a treat. When we were kids, our babysitter would take us there basically every other day, in a tango with McDonald's. I've always liked beans, but someone made fun of me for it once and I never expressed my favoritism for the vegetable again. I still get my Burrito Supreme. Daddy makes this dish called dahl, which is a type of lentil bean. Maybe that's why I like beans so much.

All eight of us feast on our respective meals. We're sitting inside the restaurant area that sits within the horseshoe shape created by the drive-thru on the outside.

As I take a bite of my burrito, Victor surmises, "I can't believe Ashar had a quintuple bypass."

Excuse me?

"No he didn't," I interject matter-of-factly. "The doctor said it was a double."

I was there. I make it a point to know everything about my family's health. You know, at least the parts they allow me to hear.

Light bulb moment.

Marci gives Victor a knowing look, to which he responds with silence. It's like he can read her mind.

"Don't worry, honey, he's doing great." She passes me some churro sticks and vanilla frosting dipping sauce. "The doctors are the best, and are taking every precaution. Your mom is with him and he's fine."

We don't get to see him until he's rested a little while. Which I get. But it doesn't appease the butterflies in my stomach, or stop them from fluttering incessantly through my intestines.

I'd be lying if I said I wasn't hurt by this withholding of information. They always do that—the protective thing. At what point does it end?

I know better than to react in any way that betrays my oscillating emotions. Plus Jenny and Andrew are around, and I don't want to worry them. I'm the big sister. I'm the example.

My appetite disappears almost instantly, like rain does when a storm wraps up its visit and moves on. One minute it's there, and the next, there's nothing but a half-eaten burrito oozing sour cream to remind you of what once was.

We're at the hospital less than three hours later. I can't think of anything but seeing my dad. Priorities take hold. Finals take a back seat in my conscious mind.

On the ninth floor, in the ICU unit, in a single room just across from the nurse's station, rests my daddy. With lines of fluids feeding into his body, he lays slightly elevated with his arms delicately folded on top of his belly. He looks sleepy. Peaceful, but sleepy.

It takes all I have to resist throwing my arms around him. He smiles at me from his bed. "How did your tests go today? Did you beat them?"

The last thing I want to talk about is my tests, and leaving my classmates in my proverbial dust. But I'm not the one that just underwent a six-hour procedure.

"I did, I beat them all."

He closes his eyes and nods, accompanied by a muted smile. I walk over to his bedside to hold his hand. He accepts my gesture and squeezes my hand. He has very soft hands. Jenny, Andrew, and Mama are there, too. We allow for each other to make our exchanges.

The surgeon, Dr. Murdock, makes his rounds. *Everything looks good,* he says. *Ashar just needs to take it easy and rest until he gets his strength back.*

I exhale in relief. Everything is temporary, including life. So fragile. I hope my dad has many more years on him. He's a young sixty-six. Having a dad that had kids later in life has its pluses and minuses.

Ryan texted me earlier to check in. We're in this limbo-y state where he hesitates about everything. He's kind of a pansy in that way. There's something missing there, something he doesn't have that I want. I'm just not sure what it is.

One thing I like about Ryan is his capacity for empathy. As an over-empathizer myself, I can appreciate a soft heart. I just wish he wouldn't cry so much. He cries more than I do. His mom probably hates that.

He knows how much my parents mean to me, even if he doesn't understand it. Sometimes I wonder if that's enough.

Chapter 34

My friend Tabatha moved to England last year with her family. Her dad had this idea to relocate across the pond for their family to experience something different. We've been friends since sixth grade, since we were both transfers to Eastcliff Elementary. Technically, everyone was new in that class; it was the first year the school opened, and there were seventeen kids in our whole class.

We're not as close as we once were, but our friendship works like that. Both our households operate on some level of paternalism, and so we share in each other's woes.

So dramatic.

When she left, Tabs invited me to visit her over Ski Week, our February break. Our school combines some of the January and February holidays into one week. It's nice to have more time to go on a trip like this one.

That week is now here, and our lives look so different. I almost decided not to go, given the current climate at Chez Selim. My parents looked at me like a Medusa personified.

"Go. You need this." Both of my parents said some version of this to me, separately. A united front.

Ryan wasn't very thrilled. He can be selfish.

Here I am, boarding my first 747 for a twelve-hour flight to the land of Cadbury chocolate and Queen (the band and the monarch). Thankfully I have a window seat in the middle-front of the main cabin. I like resting my head against the glass. I'm short, and don't need the extra legroom an aisle seat affords.

I sit next to an older man. He asks me for help filling out his customs card. His passport is green, stamped with a golden seal that includes the shape of what I can only assume to be a country, enclosed by two concentric circles. There are two languages on the front: English, and another that reminds me of but isn't quite Hindi. I learn he's from Bangladesh. I tell him my dad is from India. He says he can see it in my eyes.

We talk about travel. He lives in the U.S. now on a green card, and is on his way home to visit his family.

Daddy visits his family, too, every couple of years or so. They have never visited us in Newport. Mama says it's because they'd never leave. I'm not sure I understand what that means.

Wait, that's not true. Akram, Daddy's brother, visited for a whole year once. But that was before I was born, so it doesn't count. There are traces of him at home. Akram works in the fields; Daddy says he's really good with his hands.

His fingerprints are all over our front yard, where Mama tends her rose garden. There are plants out there that are older than I am.

Akram and Mama planted some of them together. One is a Mr. Lincoln, a shade of lipstick red. It's my favorite.

Akram is a social butterfly. He met everyone on our block and basically introduced my parents to their neighbors. Both introverts, they're not into conversation for conversation's sake. They each have their people, and each other.

Mama taught Akram how to drive. He only ever drove a tractor before that. In India, they drive on the left side of the road, like in England, a legacy of British colonization.

Speaking of England, it's my first time to Europe. It's my first time outside of the country. To think, there's so much I haven't done, seen, experienced. Compared to my elders (they would hate that term) I haven't lived a life yet. Makes my teenage drama seem so small.

An overnight flight and lots of Cheese Nips later, Heathrow appears beneath the cloud cover with mist spritzing like a steam room between heat injections.

Tabs' mom Iris picks me up from baggage claim. I always liked her. She's this lovely Belgian woman, with the kindest eyes and the biggest heart. She's the one who introduced me to chicken sandwiches from Trader Joe's. Iris is the blondest blonde, whereas Tabs is brunette. Tabs has her mom's face and her dad's color palette. Mr. Delarosa is from Guadalajara, born into a family of Tecuexe descent. The Delarosas always liked me, except maybe that one time when they found us watching the R-rated Air Force One when we were twelve years old.

"My mom lets me watch it," was my only defense. I still don't understand why it's rated R.

We truly live in a globalized world, with the opportunity to cross-pollinate everything from genes to food to disease. It's exciting and scary. Here I am, Samantha Selim, a Whindian American teenager, eating Nepalese food with a Belgian woman in a stone cottage in Surrey, England, which looks something like Kate Winslet's abode in "The Holiday."

Tabs gets home from school around four o'clock local time. Jet lag hangs heavy on my eyelids. It's eight in the morning at home. I didn't sleep much on the plane.

It's a soft exhale, seeing Tabs after so long. Or what seems like so long. Ever the adventurer, ever the challenger of the status quo, her friendship is my mirror. It's a blessing to part and pick up again as if nothing has changed.

She's a swimmer, like my siblings. Tall and lean, her figure is modelesque and toned. I thought she was shy when we first met, in sixth grade at Eastcliff. In fact, I didn't realize she was an extrovert until she met Jonah, her forbidden love. A year older than us, Jonah is brainy yet cool, fiery yet full of love. He gave her the space to be who she was.

"I can't be who I am in my family," she confided in me once. "Jonah changed everything."

Is it possible that Tabs's dad orchestrated this across the world move to pull them apart? Maybe. Or perhaps it's just a bonus. I'm sure her return home this summer will be eventful, in this context .

We gab for a few hours, over what's left of the dal bhat. Nepalese food entwines much Indian influence and is so familiar and comforting to me. Tabs asks me about Balboa Bay, my pending driver's test, Ryan.

Before this trip, I downloaded WhatsApp so Ryan and I could keep in touch. I find myself wishing I hadn't.

I've been in this country for seven hours and I already have 5 text messages and 2 missed calls. All from him.

"He's good, we're good." I can't make eye contact with her.

"Sounds like you're happy." Her forehead crinkles as she clears our dishes. Thankfully she changes the subject. "I'm so glad you're here. There's so much to see. And I'm excited for you to meet my mates—er, friends." She laughs at her word choice. "They're way different from the Cali crowd."

"Cali?" It's my turn to crinkle my forehead. Everyone knows no one from Cali actually uses the word *Cali*. "You've been gone too long."

"So my vocabulary may have changed." she pours us what's left of the mango lassi. "Change is constant, Sammy. And everything is temporary."

So wise.

Chapter 35

It's decided that I will attend classes with Tabs on Friday. It's a private school, so I need to wear their "uniform." I'm handed a tattered blazer with the school crest embroidered on the top left by a school administrator who looks like Professor McGonagall from Harry Potter. I suspect it came from the lost and found.

Tabs' older sister Dottie takes classes on a different part of the campus, since she's two years older. She's quiet, and we don't interact much. But she's nice to me.

The school day runs somewhat differently, yet somewhat the same as Balboa Bay. They have home room, which until now I've only seen in movies. They have the same classes every day, which seems like a lot. At least the periods are only 45 minutes long. And there's no time for lunch off-campus.

Introductions range from friendly to rude. There's one girl who Tabs warned me about; she has an obsession with her status as *the prettiest girl in school*. Meaning, she contours her face and wears eyeliner like Nefertiti. She's not bad looking by any means—fair skinned, with eyes the color of golden amber. Not a common combination, at least in Newport.

When she sees me, her posture relaxes noticeably, and the tautness around her mouth loosens. She stands an inch taller, nods her head in acknowledgement of me, and walks away.

Clearly she doesn't view me as any sort of competition.

"You're so pretty, you look like Moana!" a girl named Becca chants as we walk from home room to the first period. I like her.

Teenagers really are the same all over the world.

The boys remind me of characters from "Dead Poets Society." While the setting of the movie is actually not England but *New* England, I insist the parallels exist. Fresh-faced, skin as soft as Victorian upholstery, and only made human by the pink flush inflicted by the English winter air. It's not quite snowing, but the sky betrays the inception of a storm.

They are cordial and polite in their British way. I don't fancy any of them. Ha.

After school, a small group of us hits the local pub, called Cheerio. I laugh to myself. I'm kind of shocked we are going to the pub in the first place. Tabs' parents don't know. We're supposedly hanging out in the book shop by the train station before catching the last train back to Guildford.

The legal drinking age in England is eighteen, but an adult can buy alcohol for someone aged sixteen or seventeen on a licensed premises. Becca's brother John is eighteen, and knows the bar manager. How fortuitous.

Cheerio is dark and homey and accented by oak woodwork. There are etchings on the fixtures, invoking a heritage far beyond modern times. Lamplight is the only source of glow throughout the entire space. Paintings of unfamiliar faces cover the walls, sometimes broken up by a landscape or two. The ceilings are coffered, adding an element of dignity to an otherwise unremarkable space. Even so, I find it enchanting in a medieval tale kind of way. I imagine poets of the day wrote some of their great works in places like this.

We take a seat in a booth that seats six, with rich red patent leather cushions. We fit perfectly, "we" being me, Tabs, Dottie, Becca, and two other girls named Margaret and Bethany. John sits at the bar on a rickety stool chatting with the bartender. Or barman? I'm not sure what they're called here.

My grandpa owned a bar in North Dakota, way back when. I saw pictures once when we were cleaning out some old drawers. The most interesting part of the photographs is the people, standing entirely face forward, absent any smiles. My grandparents are in the photos, along with their customers. They flank the long wooden bar that runs the length of the room. Glassware hangs from the ceiling in creative arrays, not unlike in Cheerio. Two establishments miles and years away from each other, but spatially and socially? All but the same.

John brings a round of pints to our booth. Apparently *pint* is slang for *beer*, even if the amount of beer in the mug isn't a pint by volume. Ilkley Brewery's Mary Jane pale ale, that's what we're drinking. It's fresh and citric. I've never had a *craft beer* before. I haven't really had any beer before, except Bud Light sometimes when I watch football with Daddy. Battling my internal good girl, I take a few sips for show, then move on to the *chips,* i.e. french fries, radiating aromas of salt and vinegar from the center of the table.

"What do you think so far, of this little island of ours?" Becca licks her fingers clean of the salt grains between sips of her ale. Her accent transports me to the set of "The Crown."

"It's very similar to home, actually. Aside from some vocabulary and driving etiquette, it feels like I've been here before."

"You're from a beach town, right?" She looks at me with doubting eyes.

"Well, yes, that's where I grew up. I guess I mean America in general. Our east coast is very similar, places like Boston specifically. I guess that's why they call it New England."

Becca laughs, beer spraying from her nose. It's always nice when someone appreciates my sense of humor.

"Got a beau?"

A few beats of conscious silence pass before I respond. "I do, yes."

Becca waits for me to continue. When I don't, she proceeds. "I can tell your knickers never stay dry, the way you speak of him."

It's my turn to laugh. I manage a "Ha" followed by, "What makes you say that?" I'm genuinely curious. Her perspective intrigues me. It's damn near impossible to illuminate your own blind spots. You need a spotlight. Today, mine is a British teenager. What does she think?

"We're sixteen. We're at an age where love is ethereal . . ."

I like this girl, and her vocabulary.

". . . and endless. Or at least, it feels that way. Just from the three words you said about . . . I don't even know his name, which all by its lonesome is a telling sign . . . I wouldn't doubt if this love has run its course, or isn't really love to begin with, but a taste of candy . . ."

Candy? She's losing me.

". . . a sugary substitute for the real thing. While I'm sure it tingles in all sorts of places, maybe it's not love." Becca takes a sip of her ale and pauses, seemingly for effect.

"So, what I think you're saying, is I may or may not be in love, and my boyfriend tastes like candy." A burst of giggles from the rest of the table indicates some serious eaves have been dropped.

"I feel like that's a song. *My lips like sugaaahhhh* . . . or something."

Flo Rida, circa 2009.

Becca raises her glass and salutes her glass in unilateral cheers. "I could be very wrong. I just call it like I see it."

I respect that.

We arrive in Guildford on time and slightly sauced. Only slightly. I think I got lost in the gravitational pull of the rabbit hole I fell down while chatting with Becca. And forgot I was drinking. And forgot I've *never* drank.

And forgot we are under parental supervision.

Tabs is unphased by this situation. Good thing, because breaking house rules (so blatantly) is foreign to me.

I'm no angel. I recognize this. I'd like to think I'm a little more discriminating or selective when it comes to testing my boundaries. Especially when it comes to parents.

Or, more specifically, my dad.

I feel somewhat guilty, leaving the continent so soon after his surgery.

"You have only one life, Sammy. Go live it."

Ever the encouraging epithet.

For someone so protective, he sets me free.

Roots and wings.

Sometimes it feels like these things are on condition, like there's a preexisting set of terms that accompany the freedom. It's like saying, *hey, you can be free, but you have to do what I say*. Is that really freedom? Yes, I'm still a teenager. What happens when I become an adult? I guess I'll deal with that when it becomes a problem; once that bridge is built I'll strategize the hows of crossing it.

I digress.

Tabs slips me a samosa filled with garlic and onions as we walk from the train station towards her house. "Eat this, it will hide the smell and make you feel less boozy."

Where she got these I do not know, but they hit the spot.

It's before curfew, approaching 10 p.m. (Same time stateside!) Tabs' parents are in bed watching TV. We say a quick hello—the briefest of greetings—before ducking into Tabs' room. Can't imagine this isn't a regular routine.

After a soothing shower, I sleep through the sweetest slumber I've had in forever. I can't say I dream anything specific. It's more of a billowy bliss of nothing.

Chapter 36

The trip moves along in strides, filled with day trips to London, the countryside, Gloucester by the coast. It's amazing how similar and different landscapes can feel within a finite geographic space. California is like that, too. You can spend the morning surfing (or, in my case, laying) at the beach, and be boarding (or reading at the ski lodge) in the mountains by the afternoon.

My favorite day? Exploring Oxfordshire and visiting the university.

Shire is the British word for county. It reminds me of Frodo's hometown from *The Lord of the Rings*. I find history really interesting. All these old buildings make me think about the people who came before me, what they were like, how they were different, and most importantly, how they were the same. My immersion here has been enlightening in many ways. In isolation, you can only achieve so much. Our blind spots stay blind. But here, ah. Shaking up my brain cells makes for more interesting thoughts.

Oxford is the first university campus I've visited just for the sake of visiting. It's the oldest university in the English-speaking world, with evidence of teaching there dating as far back as 1096. Replete with rotundas and spires, gargoyles and grotesques, the campus and surrounding town revive a magic that seems lost yet found. Like it's sealed within the bricks and mortar—hidden, yet present.

I'm not into coffee, really, unless those spicy chai lattes from Alta count, but these cafés encourage even the bleakest believers to sip an espresso at a sidewalk bistro. I channel Gertrude Stein, complete with my copy of *The World Is Round*. I could do this for hours.

It's kind of depressing, how limited literature written for people like me, i.e. teen girls, is.

Let me rephrase. It's kind of depressing, how limited *curated* literature written for people like me, i.e. teen girls, is. Many of the books we read for English are written by white dead guys, i.e. Shakespeare, Steinbeck, Salinger. (Apparently lots of writers have last names that start with *S*.) I appreciate their works, really, I do. But the lack of representation, especially in today's world, especially in America, is kind of ridiculous.

As I sip from freshly pressed espresso, I consider how the most relatable book I've read from way back when is *Little Women*, and that wasn't even part of our curriculum. I read a children's version when I was younger, and recently reread it when the remake of the movie came out. I also read *Pride and Prejudice* for the first time when I was in fourth grade. No one believes me, but it's true. Granted, I didn't understand it the way I do now, but I think that's true of all books read and reread; you pick up different things each time.

I never really noticed it back then, the lack of range in our learning. I definitely noticed it socially, in my encounters with five-year-old girls who told me I wasn't "American," and with student teachers who couldn't give me clear direction on which EEOC box to check that would most accurately describe my hybrid heritage.

Something about this place makes me think about it in a new way.

Maybe it's because I'm beyond my previously defined boundaries. Obviously physically. But also mentally. I'm feeling different vibes. A sense of freedom I haven't felt before. I'm sure there's many reasons for that. A magic once lost yet found.

Leaving England is hard. I think the lifestyle—coffee, cafes, train rides— suits me. I might also just like being on vacation.

Between Trafalgar Square, Covent Garden, and waving to the Queen, I did manage to get some studying in. My APW textbook accounts for half of my allotted luggage weight. Upside: it helps me scale back my souvenir stash. If I had the space I'd probably buy more things than I needed. I get that from my mom's side. Not only does she have collections upon collections, but her mom accumulated an assortment of international knickknacks from her own travels. In fact, she was in Australia when she called to tell us she was sick. I picked up the phone. Didn't think it was weird she was calling from Sydney, given her penchant for jet setting.

Surprise.

I'm a little nervous to go back. Why? I have some realizations to apply. I have some people to confront. I have some books to read. I have some family to love.

I have a boyfriend . . .

Chapter 37

Daddy says he's feeling better.

Mama says she missed my puns.

Jenny, well, accuses me of stealing her AE jeans. (I didn't, they were in the washing machine.)

Andrew says he didn't notice I was gone.

Ryan says he's glad I'm home, and that he's sorry.

"For what, exactly?" This seems to be a consistent question I ask in this relationship.

"Everything." The blanket, cop-out reply that's supposed to be a sign of unconditional remorse.

My first thought: *What a lazy reply.*

Ugh. That was mean.

Chapter 38

I'm invited to a bonfire by the pier this Saturday. This time, it's Charlie I hear from.

Turns out, the FGP learned of my European Adventure—if you could even call it that. Tabs probably played up the antics on her social channels. She's a good friend like that. I suspect the invite is out of curiosity, more than anything. Maybe they are just trying to be nice? Dare I say repair our friendship?

If I'm being honest, I'm not convinced they won't do it again. It, being abandoning our friendship, forfeiting a bond to the chagrin of judgement and jealousy. And, let's face it, they're *probably* following the advice of their parents.

Just because someone is a parent doesn't mean they have all the answers.

They have the benefits of experience, sure. But even a new parent has to learn how to be a parent—they don't instantly have all the wisdom of a seasoned veteran.

Every expert was once a beginner.

School's going okay, a relative observation. Being good at school doesn't make it any more or less enjoyable. At least, not for me. It's March now, and spring is upon us.

Charlie approaches me between fifth and sixth period to make sure I'm coming to the bonfire, and to ask if I can bring marshmallows.

"Yeah, I can do that. S'mores remind me of Marshmello, and I can't imagine marshmallows without XX's where eyes would be. Damn DJ." Sometimes I'm too honest and my filter decides to, you know, not exist.

She laughs on cue, like she always did. "Sometimes I don't know where your brain comes from. That's a compliment."

I miss her. But I don't miss the pain, the abandonment.

Ryan takes me out to lunch about once a week, mostly on Fridays. This Friday, we're going to see *Little Women*. Per usual, we go to CPK for dinner before the 7 p.m.-ish screening. He hasn't heard my "representation in literature" spiel yet.

"I'm just saying," I say between bites of my BBQ chicken salad with extra herb ranch dressing, "we've had the right to vote for 100 years. At some point, doesn't anyone think it makes sense to incorporate content that represents *all* the people? After all, women are people, too. Content creation in the modern sense is somewhat new, fine, but even so, movable type was invented in the 1000s. Content, like books, poetry, love letters, has been around for at least a thousand years. Yet there's not much movement happening, or as much as we should be seeing. What about you? What's your take? Ryan? The sky's on fire!"

He's not listening. Perfect. His chin rests on his open palm, which closes around the pointy part where his three-day stubble isn't as prickly. His eyes glance down towards the food in front of him, a cheese pizza. One of the things I like about Ryan is his sophisticated palette.

After a few beats of silence, I use a spoon as a makeshift catapult to chuck a small piece of french bread (dry) at him. I target his nose, thinking it would be funny if he somehow came to consciousness just in time for the morsel to land in his mouth.

It doesn't. And he's not happy with me.

"Calm down." I sip my Shirley Temple. "You should be apologizing, not yelling at me."

"You're the one that threw food in my face, *babe*." I hate it when he says *babe* like that, as though using the title somehow entitles him to certain behaviors.

Newsflash: it doesn't.

"You're right. I should be disciplined. Nevermind that you're the one who ignores me anytime we start a conversation about feminism. Apparently that's one of the topics that is off-limits."

When we first started dating, we had a conversation about what we'll call "sensitive topics." They're not off-limits, per se, but they're the kinds of conversations that may lead to disagreements or heated debate at the very least. Basically anything political or religious. And apparently, feminist. I guess you could call them hot button topics, depending on the audience.

He's quiet now.

Sometimes I think he lives in his own world. I guess most people do, since perception is reality. I give him credit for choosing me. But I'm starting to suspect his reasons for that are not as well-intentioned as I imagined. That's got to be some sort of psychological thing: that if you like something about someone, you're more likely to assume you'll like other things about them too, that they're good all around. What an impossible standard. That's my bad for assuming.

"I feel like I spend more time apologizing to you than anything else."

That's probably the most honest thing he's said to me in a while.

"Go on." I genuinely want him to go on.

He eyes me. He's probably wondering if it's a trick.

"Sounds like a trick." He laughs, heartily and with gusto. One of the things I like most about Ryan is his laugh. It's probably the most honest thing about him.

"I guess, I'm feeling that . . . well . . . we're just not . . . clicking? . . . for some reason . . ." His voice punches and lingers at the same time, like a speedboat making sharp turns and leaving a frothy wake.

"And I don't know why, exactly."

"Well," I venture, "our lifestyles are different now than when we first started dating. You're in college now. You have . . . freedoms . . . that I just don't. Do you think that's part of it?" I pause. "Maybe I'm holding you back?"

I've never verbalized it before, this concern. Mostly because I don't think it's true. But I'm wondering what truth he finds in it. I guess it's only fair.

"I don't think that's it."

Phew.

"I feel like I'm disappointing you."

"Disappointing me? What does that even mean?"

I feel my cheeks rise in temperature.

"Like I'm not meeting the standard you have for our relationship, or something."

Or something? That's helpful. I had no idea this kid was so insecure.

I can see tears pooling in his eyes. See, he cries all the time.

"So this is my fault? You feeling like you're not *enough*, or whatever?"

"No, I—I—didn't say that—"

"This is a relationship, Ry. It takes two to tango. It feels like you're more interested in performing a soliloquy, which we both know you're sooooo good at."

That was kinda mean. I think back to drama class and my first impression of him then, answering our teacher's question like he was giving a speech. There are always signs if you care to see them.

"You're right." He says that a lot. "I'm sorry. Can we just forget it? I didn't get enough sleep, and it's almost time for the movie."

He does that a lot, the cop out. We'll never finish this particular conversation, the one where he reveals his insecurity around disappointing me. I'm sure that was hard for him to do. I wonder, though, if I'm just not giving him enough attention? Maybe it's the sex thing? Maybe I'm still mad at him for the Lucie thing? (Obviously I still am.)

But is that fair? What's *fair*?

I feel guilty. I'm not sure why, though. I hear my internal dialogue reference names like Dustin, Cameron, but I quickly bury them under Ryan's accusatory comments. There are always layers, and I always start at the surface. That makes the most sense, right? Important to establish footing, bearings, then penetrate.

Are we spending too much time at the surface? Are we dancing instead of digging? Maybe.

Better get the shovel.

"Okay, we can finish this later."

We won't, but that's okay. I'll begin the excavation process soon. But tonight we're watching *Little Women* and validating Jo March's writing ambitions.

Chapter 39

I'm not sleeping well tonight. I don't think it's because of whatever that exchange was with Ryan. An argument? A fight? It didn't carry the punch of anything like that. A disagreement? That seems half-hearted. It was more like a playful prodding gone wrong, that escalated into a more serious conversation, with more remaining said than addressed.

Is there a word for that?

Ryan aside, my mind turns over in anticipation of the bonfire. Why? I'm almost certain Cameron will be there.

I can't explain what it is, this feeling, this pang of hope. It's not like I'm planning on cheating on my boyfriend. It's nothing as sinister, as conniving, as that. It's a reciprocity, a mutual understanding of attraction I want. From someone *other* than my boyfriend. Is that fair? What's fair? A common theme, lately.

Ah, yes—the omnipresent duality of hope and fear. *May your choices reflect your hopes, not your fears.* A favorite quote of mine.

But what if your hope could be construed as unethical? What do you say to that, Mr. Mandela? Probably that ethics are a given assumption to that statement. But I think it's worth asking.

This is probably something that should be debated in a philosophy class. I don't think they offer that at Balboa Bay. Maybe they should.

I digress.

My dreams are mostly made up of revisionist experiences. Meaning, I relive things that happen to me in my dreams, but with alternative nuances. Like I'm rewriting what happens in reality, and this alternative reality only exists in my subconscious, in my personal nighttime world. Only my eyes are closed, and the only thing actively in play is my imagination.

Most times, I recreate encounters I wish had played out differently. I can be pretty quippy in the moment, but sometimes I come up with even *better* responses after the fact. In my dreams, I have an opportunity to play them out on my own terms.

That sounds like a control thing. Power and control are such human matters. I'm not exempt from that. Really, what matters (ha) is how you manifest it, how you harness it for the positive, for the good.

From where I'm sleeping, I don't think I'm doing a good job right now.

Because the content of my dreams tonight is centered around Cameron, the Duffy, and our moments alone.

Nothing inappropriate happens, though. In my dreams.

Chapter 40

The fire pits are about a mile south of my house. I could walk there if I wanted to.

The pits flank Balboa Pier on the north and south sides. There are parking lots on both sides, at M, A, and B Streets. There are towers there, too. Ryan works at A Street sometimes, but not often. That's where all the groms go to skimboard.

We used to frequent the playground next to junior guard headquarters at B Street. My favorite piece of equipment, if you could call it that, was an old water pipe about five feet in diameter that just sat in the sand behind the swingset. We would use charcoal we found in the sand (don't know where it came from) to write our names and other things on the inside of it. It's since been removed.

I write on everything. When I was learning the alphabet, I would write, *in pen*, on my bedroom walls. Even after significant scrubbing, you can still see traces of the As and Hs, my favorite letters.

Mama drops me off right after sunset, which at this time of year is around 7 p.m. In the maybe ten minutes it takes to get from our house to the parking lot next to the bonfire, Mama shines a few of her wisdom pearls in my face.

"Is Ryan coming tonight?"

"I saw him last night, Mama." It comes out in one breath, sounding like all one word.

"I know, just curious. Who will be there tonight?"

"Charlie, Alex, some people from Cove High—"

"Cameron?"

I hate it when she does that.

"Maybe, I don't know for sure." Though secretly hoping. "I haven't talked to him since Alex's holiday party."

"Does Ryan know about Cameron?"

Sometimes I tell her things against my better judgement.

"I'm not sure."

A heavy silence follows. Only Zac Brown Band's "Goodbye In Her Eyes" is audible, playing from the car speakers. Nice, Universe.

"Okay, hun. I know you love him. But sometimes, love is temporary."

"You're not talking about Cameron, are you." Definitely a statement, not a question.

She reintroduces the silence. Sometimes a thoughtful pause is all you need.

There's already a decent number of people there by the time we pull up to the curb. I see Charlie and Alex sitting on beach towels and chatting together amongst a mix of people I know and people I don't. *Know* is defined loosely here, as in I'm aware of their existence. Who really knows anyone, anyway? We all keep secrets, even when we don't mean to.

Mellows and towel in tow, I say bye to Mama and approach the group solo. Arriving alone to a bonfire isn't as awkward as arriving alone to a house party. The entry to a house party is a bottleneck, whereas to a bonfire it's more like a roundabout.

Charlie sees me when I'm about twenty feet away. She smiles delicately, almost naturally, before she starts walking toward me.

"Sammy! You made it!" She embraces me, as friends might, before taking a step back to acknowledge the moment.

"C'mon, you know I love a good bonfire. The smoky smell on my clothes afterwards is the sign of a good time." She knows I hate the smell.

She laughs, because she knows.

"I'll take those from you," she says as she plucks the bag of marshmallows from my hand. "We have this pit over here. Do you know everybody?"

I skim the mishmash of tortured teens surrounding the burning ring of fire. Remarkably, I recognize all the faces. Shocking. Mostly Cove kids, which is probably for the better. My identity with this group is much more fluid.

I nod the affirmative to Charlie, as we join the dozen or so people already present. Mostly dudes. The girls know better, to arrive fashionably late. I don't like arriving late; I find it causes more attention.

"Hey chica." Alex comes over to me and gives me a hug. It feels real, authentic and loving. Still, I question it. Wounds are still fresh, one year later. Even salt couldn't heal this one.

"Hey girl, how are you?" A loaded question but a safe, small talk greeting.

"Good, I'm good. Swim's back in season, so that keeps me busy. How's Ryan?"

I honestly haven't prepared to answer this question. Not that I should have to, but it's always easier when you're prepared.

"He's good, he likes college." Did I have to rub it in that I'm dating a college guy? "We saw *Little Women* last night." No one probably cares, but I'm hoping to change the subject.

"Oh, I've been wanting to see that! What did you think of it?" Charlie, my fellow feminist.

"I enjoyed it overall. Great script, strong characters, for the most part. I think I like the 90s version better though. This one jumped around a lot in terms of flashbacks. And I wasn't a hundred percent sold on the casting. I think Winona Ryder made a stronger Jo. That's probably the part that disappointed me the most. But it was well done. I think it's just a matter of preference."

"That sucks the lead was disappointing, though."

"Me too. For some reason I didn't feel a sense of conviction from her, you know? Like Winona, you could tell she was fierce. This one was more delicate, which is also fine. In a way it's kind of nice to see two totally different versions of the same character accomplish similar goals. Like, you can achieve something if you want to even if it's not totally obvious that someone should be something. It's internal."

I draw blank stares.

Followed by a "Daaaaaang, that's deep!" from someone I know but don't really know.

I'm blushing just a little, but it's mostly dark now and our only source of light is the kindle from the bonfire.

"What's deep?"

Uh oh.

I know that voice. It's husky, somewhat gruff, but also just a little post-pubescent.

Cameron.

He speaks from behind me, and I do my best not to cause myself any whiplash by turning around too quickly. Or give any indication of my thumping heart.

Luckily, Alex responds for the group.

"Sam was just giving us her review of *Little Women*. Have you seen it?"

"The chick flick? Nah. I'm more of a Marvel kind of guy."

'Yeah, *Wonder Woman* is legit." I can't help myself.

I see him smile; it's tight-lipped. We make eye contact, then he blinks. And our moment is over.

Way over.

He makes his rounds, and I busy myself with skewering marshmallows. Preoccupying my hands tends to busy my brain, distracting it from other thoughts and keeping the pit of my stomach out of my scope of awareness.

Cameron and I don't speak the rest of the night. But I'm very aware of his whereabouts.

First, after making his rounds and saying hi to everyone, he finds a seat next to his homie from Cove High. They chat for a good half hour.

Enter Lucie.

She's wearing dark denim that looks like it's painted on, with a black long-sleeve yet sheer top equally as tight. She's one of the leanest water polo players I've ever seen.

She must be cold.

I, in contrast, am wearing my black Jack's Surfboards hoodie and boyfriend jeans. Not exactly slimming. But definitely more beach appropriate. Boys know nothing of these things. I probably should have gone with something more fitted. Mental note.

Eventually, I see Cameron take off his token black zip-up and wrap it around Lucie's shoulders.

What is this feeling, my heart plunging towards my pelvis, like it's weighing anchor?

I try not to look, but the visual makes my eyes burn, like when you're cutting onions: You want to look away, but you can't because you have to continue chopping until you have enough diced pieces for the tikka masala.

To be honest, it's probably also the embers from the fire. One switch of wind and you're done for. Usually I'm better about being aware of this stuff. But tonight, I'm on a different plane of pain.

Pain. That's what it feels like. Brutal, sharp, shallow bursts of pain. I imagine this is something of what going into labor feels like. Menstrual cramps are bad enough.

I sip a solo cup of 7Up, trying to make conversation with a Cove girl about nail polish colors. When I mention the color wheel, she stares at me blankly.

"Pastels. This time of year I like to wear a lot of pastels. Essie has some great ones."

She smiles at that. I can be relatable.

Out of the corner of my eye, I see two people, a couple, removing themselves from the bonfire revelry. An inverted silhouette. Long blonde hair is tucked between the back of her hoodie and the hood itself. He's in a white button down with no outerwear to speak of.

Oh.

I know.

They're going off to be alone. Because they can. Unattached. Unabating. Undeceiving. Because I can't. Because I'm tethered.

Then I am sad. Just sad. Left out, maybe?

But then it clicks, like a locker combination.

Lucie and Cameron are free. And I am not.

I watch them, dizzy in their newfound, daze-y romance. If you could call it that, romance. Maybe it will be a one-night love affair. Maybe it's the start of a lifetime of bliss.

In my envy, I pull out my phone and consult the screen.

Nothing.

My sadness becomes loneliness, the FOMO kind. It's separation, it's isolation, it's a siloed sorrow bordering on despair.

Hormones—the things that bring us ecstasy—are the same arbiters of our pain.

My role in all of this?

Participatory, yes. But why do I feel this way? This sadness?

Self-inflicted? Maybe.

I'm not trying to be a bad, unethical person. I'm not malicious and don't wish harm on others. I just don't do that.

Then why do I feel so bad?

Guilt? Maybe.

I guess I'm not the only one that craves validation. Is that what this is?

I just want peace. Freedom.

The fire burns my face. I'm sitting too close. It returns the feeling to my body.

I'd say it's the cold that invites the numbness.

But we know that's not the truth.

Chapter 41

On my sixteenth birthday, I fail my driver's test. The examiner says my driving is "dangerous." Direct quote. I may have cut someone off as we were leaving the DMV parking lot. Doomed from the start.

My impatience shows up at some really inopportune times.

We reschedule the test for three weeks later, per the retake protocol.

I'm not super depressed about it or anything. It's more of an inconvenience. I definitely don't consider my birthday to be ruined. I'm not that dramatic.

Ryan has class at one, so he can't take me to lunch. Mama feels bad for me failing the test, so I don't go back to class anyway and we go to lunch at Joe's Crab Shack on the water.

It's become our go-to spot for midday treats, whenever they do happen. Such as after the district spelling bee in fifth *and* sixth grade. Both were consolation lunches; I lost both times to the *same girl* from Whittier.

I sense a theme.

My losing words were *moccasin* and *insatiable*. I'll never forget how to spell those words ever again.

The servers have this bit where if you're celebrating something, they make (ask?) you to wear a goofy sombrero and poncho while taking a lap through the aisles of the tables and booths.

I didn't think they'd insist I participate, given my recent success at the spelling bee.

They did.

Today we don't tell them it's my birthday. I'm not feeling poncho-worthy.

That evening we have a nice dinner at home: short ribs mixed on the stove top with onions, garlic, tomato, and spinach, accompanied by rice and/or naan, and a side salad with bleu cheese dressing. The grande finale is carrot cake with walnut cream cheese frosting from French's Cupcake Bakery, where we've been getting our birthday and occasion cakes since Jenny's first birthday.

We used to have dinner at the dining room table every night when we were kids. My job was to set the table. Jenny and Andrew didn't have jobs. Again, being the oldest, I usually get saddled with responsibilities first, and if there's anything left over, they handle those. Now that we're older, i.e., that Sis and I are in high school, our schedules are all over the place. Yoga for me, soccer for her, baseball for Andrew (basketball is over, and by extension so is Dustin)—not to mention school projects and duh, studying, the latter of which probably takes the most precedence in our house.

Now, the dining room table is an ode to work ethic. Daddy uses it until 1 p.m. for his charting. Mama has her spot on the opposite corner, where she reads the paper and sips her morning coffee. The rest of it plays host to our textbooks and homework.

Up until a few years ago, we shared one desktop computer. *All five of us*. It happened to live in *my* bedroom. Apparently there was no better place to put it. (Backstory: my bedroom used to be Daddy's office. When I moved in, we left the computer desk there, because there was no better place to put it. Funny, how underlying issues pervade when not addressed from the outset.) You can imagine the foot traffic in and out.

I spent, past tense, a lot of time on Gchat chatting with my girlfriends. Andrew plays those brainless video games. I don't know what Jenny does; she's very private. Daddy checks his stock quotes at all hours, since we live in a world where, at any given time across the globe, money is changing hands. I'd wake up to the glow of the computer screen most nights, but I dealt with it. Mama uses her cell phone for all her web-related needs.

Eventually, we convinced our parents to invest in laptops—the pinnacle of independence and mobility, as far as we're concerned. But first I negotiated a trade to encourage a revision to the thinking around this particular circumstance. Downstairs, in our family room, photo albums occupied valuable real estate. I proposed we relocate the albums to my room, in exchange for moving the computer workstation to the family room. Which now, in hindsight, makes total sense. Really, I was the losing party in all of this, defaulting me to presenting any alternative, if any. Just took me a bit to find the solution. And to wait to actually see the change through. That was probably the hardest part. Inertia is a condition of change.

The lesson? Baby steps. A good example of my learned patience. Though I still need work on that. Just ask anyone in my family.

After cake, it's just about time for *Jeopardy!* to start. This week is the teacher's tournament. For some reason, I get more questions right during this particular segment of shows than during any other time. I wonder why that is? Maybe I'm just more in sync with those writers than others.

I'm grateful for an early night. Well, earlier than usual. I could use some time alone with my thoughts. I don't get enough of that.

Happy birthday to me.

Chapter 42

Around 9 p.m., Ryan shows up with roses.

There's a card, too, with a poem. We haven't written poems in a while, at least not to each other. They wouldn't be as lovey as last year's. At least not from me. I feel like that would mean something.

This poem is short, a haiku actually.

He's never written me a haiku before.

What does that mean?

Everything, and nothing.

Birthday kisses, yum.

Another year lived for you.

Happy birthday, Boo.

Yum? How romantically poetic. Everything I ever dreamed of as a commemoration of my sixteenth birthday.

My mom gave me a heart-shaped pendant necklace engraved with the date and my name. Jewelry always wins.

Although, I do like flowers. Who doesn't like getting flowers? Peonies are my favorite in terms of aesthetics. I've also always loved carnations; they last *forever*. Gardenia is my favorite scent of all time. Gardenias are bushes, and therefore difficult to incorporate into an arrangement.

Roses are nice, too. Tried and true. I have a soft spot for roses. Mama has been growing roses since she and Daddy moved into the house all those years ago. I mentioned the bush that she and Akram planted when he came to visit, the Mr. Lincoln—the deepest red of rose I've ever seen. This was pre-Sammy, Jenny, and Andrew. It's nice that he's present here in some way.

A farmer by trade, Akram is also a great cook. Mama talks about how Akram taught her to make Indian dishes like saag and aloo gobi. They rival Daddy's curry in taste and texture. A practicing Muslim, Akram only eats blessed meat. Eventually, given the closest imam lived in Garden Grove, Akram started performing his own prayers.

Mama also taught Akram how to drive. Sounds like he learned pretty quickly. She says teaching him wasn't any harder than teaching me. What a relief. He probably wasn't considered "dangerous." I will own that title forever.

I digress.

Ryan's roses—not to be confused with Seacrest's morning segment on KISS FM—are nice. They're this deep pink, vibrant and velvety. I like them, really I do. Compared to other gifts, they're just not as thoughtful.

Am I a bad person for thinking that?

He senses something wrong. Pun intended.

"You don't like them? I know you love it when I bring you flowers."

I think for a few beats before responding.

"I do. But it's my birthday . . . so I guess I just thought . . . that . . . maybe you would have thought of something . . . more . . ." I search for the word and come up empty.

"Thoughtful?" Meek and muffled, I wouldn't recognize his voice if he weren't standing in front of me.

It sounds bad, but that's how I feel. I'm accusing my boyfriend of not being thoughtful. On my birthday. Who dictates what *thoughtful* is, anyway? How do other couples define it? We can't be the first pair of teenagers asking this question.

Mama says events can bring out stressors that are otherwise hidden. Birthdays count, even if there isn't an actual *event*. It's a life event, like losing your first tooth or starting your first job. I mean, I am sweet sixteen.

Though it doesn't really feel that sweet. It's more salty, actually.

"Yeah, I guess that's what I mean."

"Oh. Okay." The -ay echoes through the alley, where we're standing. It's empty, aside from us and the trash bins waiting to be collected in the morning.

We're standing a few feet apart, bathed in the glow of the outdoor lamps that are attached to the side of the house. They remind me of the lampposts in "Peter Pan", the Disney cartoon. Why that sticks out to me, I don't know.

Ryan shuffles a bit, shifting his weight in his Rainbow-clad feet. His Quiksilver hoodie looks cropped on his long torsoed body. His gaze is down. One of the things I don't like about Ryan is how he practically hides from me when we're having a conversation when it's not a positive one.

It's kind of spineless. He leaves his backbone in the lineup, when his wave gets snaked and he has an endless string of colorful words for the offender.

Me? I get silence and a solemn stare towards my knees.

"I feel like I'm always disappointing you, Sam."

Ughhhhhhh.

WE'VE BEEN OVER THIS.

How is this even productive?

I feel this, he says. *I feel that*, he whines. I get it. You have feelings. So how do we address them?

"What does that even mean?" My best attempt at addressing them. Flashbacks to our dinner at CPK fill my prefrontal cortex. My brain hosts an internal competition for what pithy remark to shell out next.

I'm holding the bouquet like a baby cooing in a lullaby. All I really want to do is chuck them at his face. But I'm mature, so I don't.

As if this conversation is any indication.

"I feel like you're punishing me." He stops moving, eyes piercing blue—a beautiful blue—illustrating his own belief in his words, even if their roots in reality are tenuous at best.

Yet there it is. Plain as day, dark as the night surrounding us.

"For . . ."

I want to hear him say it.

"C'mon Sam, you know."

"I want to hear you say it."

A few asana breaths later, I hear a tight squeak. "For hanging out with Lucie."

Ugh.

"Right." I set the bouquet down on top of the trash bins for safekeeping. Foreshadowing much? "I'm punishing you for hanging out with Lucie? If that's the version of the truth you're going with, I have nothing more to say to you."

Hopeful, perhaps mistakenly so, I leave the space between us hollow for him to fill. With a second chance. With a kiss. With an act of valor.

He doesn't.

So I go.

I leave the flowers.

Behind me I hear him shuffle again, pacing as he does when he's nervous. I move quickly through the wooden gate and back patio, into the house and behind the protection of the sliding glass door.

I stand, alone, absorbing the weight of the moment.

When I realize he's not following me, I cry a little.

For what?

For his insensitivity? For his lack of thoughtfulness? For his blatant disregard for the truth?

Having a boyfriend is hard.

Not that I'm the greatest girlfriend on the planet.

At least I didn't show up on the night he turned sixteen and make him cry.

Chapter 43

Ryan calls me a few times the next day.

He never calls. He's a texter. It's one of the (apparently many) points of contention in our relationship.

"I'm sorry, I didn't mean to be so thoughtless. This was your sixteenth birthday, and I should have been more on top of it. I thought you liked roses, and my thought process ended there. You know we've been together for so long I'm running out of ideas of what to get you."

It would have been sweet if he wasn't so honest.

"It's okay. I'm sorry for getting mad."

All we do is apologize to each other. What does that say about our relationship?

AP exams start next week. Mine is on the first Wednesday of the two-week schedule. There are two exams a day. Classes for the rest of the school continue as usual. Can't wait until next year, when, if things go according to plan, I'll have three to take. I'm ready, despite everything. Relationships are so distracting. My revisionist dreams have increased in frequency over the past few weeks. More macro, though, which is different from the usual dialogue rewrites. Right now, my dreams are revising entire periods of time. What does that mean?

World History is such a broad topic, and I knew that at the beginning of the year. Now nearing the finish line of the curriculum, I can affirm this more than ever. The teacher says there's a strategy for taking the test, and that's what he's tried to prepare us for with his exams and assignments.

I personally don't see it.

Ancient civilizations are the most interesting to me. They're foundational. I also like patterns, seeing recurring themes throughout human lives. But I guess most subjects are like that. History is the most obvious one. But take English, for example. Books by Jane Austen talk about the same themes as books by Elizabeth Acevedo: youth, love, family dynamics. Though they transcend time and culture, their messages resonate with their readers. They're relatable. How beautiful is that? We're all connected through our stories regardless of where and when we come from. Mind. Blown.

We just don't get to dive as deeply into these patterns until college, I can only assume. We definitely don't get to in these classrooms.

At least with these exams, there's a writing component. Writing exams afford some liberties. You can sound like you know what you're talking about, when you might not have the faintest idea. If you include enough details about this war or that emperor, you might be able to get by. This approach has personally never worked for me. I like to know what I'm writing about. Otherwise, it's phony. Like greasy salespeople. I don't like greasy salespeople. Charm only gets you so far. I also like to get good, no, *great* grades. But not at the expense of being dishonest. Because that's what it feels like to me. Dishonesty. If I don't know the answer, I don't know the answer. If I don't know the answer, I'll learn it and move on. School is about measuring the things we know at any given moment. I like the thrill of it all, competing against myself and others. I haven't really thought about school for school's sake. I just like exercising my brain.

When it comes down to it, it's all strategy. You just have to figure out what works for you.

Ryan never took an AP class. They never motivated him, he says. He always planned to go to junior college first and figure out what he likes, before committing to studying something he wasn't sure he even likes.

Sound logic. There's so much pressure, from so many different angles. Parents. Teachers. Friends. Society. It's manipulative: *Follow your dreams! As long as they're consistent with our expectations of you.* Expectations are debilitating if they're not clear or consistent. Especially for young adults. Our brains are still forming, and we have enough literal growing pains as it is.

Ryan's brain is still growing, too. He does have a gift for words. His vocabulary makes me smitten. Though it hasn't made many appearances lately. His tear ducts are probably requiring more of his attention lately. I really don't mind that he cries. I think more men should cry. It's healthy and healing. I just don't like how he uses it as a crutch to make me feel sorry for him. That's not productive or fair.

After school, we text a while, Ryan and I. My attention turns from Zheng He to this weekend's epic swell, then back to China's global empire. I'm a solid multitasker. Balancing schools and relationships is consuming for all parties involved. The key is how you manage it.

Chapter 44

I pass my driver's test retake. I forget to call Ryan.

Chapter 45

So many tests. No wonder us kids feel like we're always being judged. Because we are always being judged.

The APW exam is long and calorie-burning. My blood sugar drops with every multiple choice question answered or skipped. They actually deduct points if you answer a question wrong. What kind of grading scale is that? Not one that encourages or supports risk.

There are ninety multiple choice questions and three essays. I hydrate as often as possible. I also eat pieces of chocolate, Cadbury specifically, during breaks. The powers of chocolate cannot be underestimated. I suspect it's the cacao.

These tests are graded on a curve. It's hard to know how well I did. I know at least seventy percent of the multiple choice questions. The essays—one about Mesoamerica, one compare/contrast of Vietnam and Great Britain, and one about sub-saharan Africa—are manageable. I'm not sure my arguments are steel strong, but I include a crap ton of detail. We'll see how that serves me.

We get our scores over the summer. Something to look forward to.

My chest is still tight, even after this.

Our exam ends around 11 a.m., and it's Wednesday. Meaning, after lunch, we have sixth period for two hours.

I hear the thudding of a would-be hockey player loitering just past the entryway of the classroom. I learned that Mark blew out his knee during a hockey tournament. He doesn't play competitively anymore.

"Did you get an A-plus-plus?" Mark's enthusiasm for my academic performance always amazes me. Even from across the room, he leaves his indelible mark on my day.

"Yes, in fact I think I pulled an A-plus-plus-plus."

"I'm sure the graders will be swept away by your extensive lexicon. They'll probably think a bot took the test. That's how good you did."

"Do you even know what a lexicon is?"

"I feel like you're insulting my intelligence right now."

"I feel like you're consciously avoiding answering my question."

"Well, yes. Next question."

My eyeballs roll towards the back of my head just as the teacher begins the lecture on poetry. Mark and I don't talk much anymore. I actually miss our banter about everything and nothing. Guess Miss Wally's antics worked.

"In our last new lesson of the semester, we'll learn about poetry and the various devices used in poetry to convey ideas, themes, and emotions. For the concluding project, you'll each choose a theme and curate a collection of poems, using the criteria outlined in this rubric." She passes a handout to each side of the classroom.

I hate it when school intersects with real life. It makes things way more complicated than they need to be. The last thing I want to do is write poetry for *school*. Poetry reminds me of Ryan, of the beginning of our relationship. It represents our bond. Dissecting it with literary devices kills it. Death by diction.

After class, I visit my locker to deposit some papers before heading out to the pool parking lot to meet my mom. Inside my locker is a flyer for *Harpoon*. Applications are being accepted, it says. For those interested in writing and learning about media and publishing.

Eh, the media. Given the current landscape of our country, the media holds a contradictory position in my mind. Information is so ubiquitous, fact checking all but absent. Anything printed or posted inherently holds truth. It's exhausting not only harvesting the information but sowing the seeds. What happened to responsible reporting? Sensationalism shakes up the sense of right and wrong. It shouldn't be this hard for people to understand the facts and make up their own minds about the truth.

After all, truth is personal.

But fact is fact. Stories are human constructs to explain ideas, themes, and emotions. Stories illustrate truth. But they can also be fiction. Adults think teens are impressionable. But adults are the ones who believe anything they read.

"You love writing, Sam." Mama states the obvious when I disclose my limited interest in joining the staff. Sometimes the obvious statements are necessary. Sometimes the deliverer is more important than the message itself. "What other opportunities do you have to write for fun?"

"Um, well, there's my journals, that's fun I guess."

"Your journals are great, and you should continue to write in them. You know, John Steinbeck based his own books off of his personal journals." This is probably the ninth time I myself can count she has referenced Steinbeck's commitment to documenting his own history. "One day you could write a book about your own life. But right now, it might be good for you to write about stuff that's not so personal, too."

I noodle on that for a moment.

"You have so much to say—"

"Are you saying I'm too chatty?"

She looks at me like only a mother can look at a daughter.

"Sorry." I'm ashamed.

"I'm saying you have a lot of thoughts and observations about the world, and this could be a good opportunity for you to share them and learn more about the industry along the way."

She's soooooooo wise. As a multitasker, I can appreciate killing multiple pigeons with one oversized stone. Leaves more time for yoga, and who are we kidding: boy trouble.

It's decided. I will apply for a spot on the *Harpoon* staff. The process seems kind of rigorous: in addition to a written application, prospects are required to participate in a two-hour-long article writing exercise on campus in the Mac Lab. The idea is for the editors to get a sense for writing style in a timed setting, with limited access to additional resources. (Who are we kidding though, the internet is all you really need for something like this.) I can appreciate the spirit of what they're trying to accomplish. How else can you really assess someone's writing ability, without certain advantages afforded by technology? Spellcheck is one thing, but creating your own IP is a whole other animal. Unless you plagiarize. That's just stealing. Thankfully there's turnitin.com to deter those tempted.

Finals are coming, too, like a roadster taking the hard right down PCH from West Newport towards the peninsula. I'm not too worried about them. Now that APW is all but out of the way, I can focus on closing the year out with a bang.

Beth tries to claim rights to be my study partner for the French final. Since the Ryan-Lucie reveal, she's been extra nice. Seems fake to me. Like because she told me about their jacuzzi jam session, she owes me.

I don't see it that way.

Todd needs some help with geometry. That'll be a piece of carrot cake.

Speaking of Ryan (I'm backtracking), his exams are over next week. College kids, what a life. They have half as much class time and shorter semesters by at least five weeks.

And Tabs comes back in two weeks! Her time abroad hovers over this year like benchmark events in my own life. I'm glad she's coming back.

Chapter 46

I didn't think the application process would be so stressful.

Correction: I *hoped* the application process wouldn't be so stressful. Sitting in a room behind desktops with forty other people, typing in silence, vying for twenty spots, is downright intimidating.

The initial written part wasn't so bad: just your typical personal information and general essays, such as W*hy do you want to be a member of* Harpoon?, *Describe your writing style, and What ideas do you have to improve the publication?* They're just looking for some free feedback with that last one. Can't blame them.

That initial part serves as the ticket to today's timed section. Literally. You bring a printed version of your responses with you to the door, hand it to one of the future editors (his name is Tobin, I think), and he points you to a seat in one of the ten rows of seating. We're spaced out at every other computer. Why, I don't know. To protect against cheating? Maybe it's for comfort? Spatial juju?

Whatever the case, I'm assigned to a spot next to the far wall so I only have one neighbor to my left.

"Good luck," he says to me, "these prompts are tough."

How would he know? We've been told not to turn over the paper with the prompts until "go time."

Obviously he peeked. Why does it still surprise me when people cheat. (Statement, not a question.)

I realize he's trying to psych me out. Please, brosky, I could write a paper about (almost) anything in my sleep.

"They're probably looking for us to format our content in AP style, too." The color drains from his face. I'm so bad. I totally knew he wouldn't know what that is. At least there's the internet; he can Google it after he regains his composure. "Good luck," I hiss, flashing my most charming smile.

When it's officially time to start, I review the prompts, all three of them, and take a deep breath. Sometimes I forget to breathe in stressful situations. It's amazing how breathing keeps us alive.

These aren't hard. The first asks for a news article about a current event. Straightforward. The second asks for a feature on a person you consider a mentor or advisor. A little harder, but doable. The third asks for a column/opinion piece about school dress codes. I stifle a laugh. Are we really still talking about dress codes at BBHS? *Maybe that's the point!* Perhaps my position will be related to geography, zip codes, what dress codes achieve and how they help or harm a school. This will be a fun rabbit hole!

Said no one ever.

We have two hours to crank out these stories. The directions don't say anything about using AP Style. And I don't want to be that girl that asks. I've noticed that when girls ask questions, we're considered dumb—like, *Duh, why did she have to ask that? The answer is SO obvious!* (That's the not-so-subconscious reason why I don't ask questions in class.) Yet when boys ask the same question, they're considered intelligent questions—like *wow, good job for noticing that gap in the instructions!* It's not the boys' fault, though, that's unconscious bias.

"Should we be using AP Style for these stories?" Guess who asks this?

The guy on my left. Let's call him Lefty.

"Not necessary, unless you feel like it helps you. Thanks for asking." At least Tobin's reply is diplomatic.

Lefty smirks at me before the pitter-patter of his keyboard escalates from a melodious series of taps to an assault on QWERTY. I, for the most part, mind my own business and get to work.

I choose the healthcare crisis as my current event. So much fact-based stuff to talk about. My mentor is my mom (duh). Well, both my parents, really, but if I had to pick one, walking the plank, it would be my mom. I have the column concept in the bag.

I finish in under an hour and a half. I close the windows on my computer after printing and emailing my finished articles. I'm confident, even though I'm still nervous for the pending judgement of my qualifications as a BBHS *Harpoon* staffer. I'm proud of my output.

As I get up to leave, Lefty has beads of sweat rolling down a pulsating vein that's nearly popping out of his neck. *AP Style can't save you now, asshole.*

There's maybe ten people that finish before me. I'm okay with that. I question myself a lot when I'm one of the first to finish. Is it me doubting my abilities? Maybe. I'm also less patient than the average human. So I always check my work, then turn in my assignments. Today was no different.

I drop my paperwork into the bin next to the door, sign my name on the checkout sheet, and proceed on my way. Not before I all but whisper, "Thanks for the opportunity," to Tobin. Sounds formal, but I'd rather be too formal than too casual. He smiles gently, like he's reading the *oh shit* expression on my face.

It's almost four-thirty. Daddy picks me up today. I asked him to be here at five because that's the latest I'd be out.

He's already here. Always early. I'm relieved, actually. And tired. Writing is exhausting. It burns a lot of calories. Writing is exercise. I mean, the brain is also a muscle. People forget that sometimes.

"How did it go? Did you give it to them?" Direct and to the point.

"I think I did good, Daddy. I should know if I made it soon."

And we sit in silence the rest of the drive home, appreciating each other's company.

Chapter 47

Tabs
*Can we meet at your house? My
parents don't want me driving in cars
with boys.*

Sam
*Sure. what are you telling them we're
doing?*

Tabs
*Biking to the beach and hanging out
by your place. Is that cool? Sellable?*

Sam

*Haha def sellable. We can park our
bikes at the pier and have the guys
pick us up there. That work?*

Tabs

*Brill ! you know how to make it work.
be down there by 11 latest.*

I swear, in every high school class, there's one guy that has a black suburban (or some close equivalent) who basically acts like the designated Uber XL driver for the whole crew. Our class has one too. His name is Derek Buckingham.

For Jonah's group, it's Tatum Turbo. What a great name for a running back.

Between Tabs and me, we know how to cover our bases. England makes for its own shenanigans, but Newport is a whole other animal.

When you manage to keep a relationship hidden from at least one parent for the better part of two years, you earn a certain reputation for figuring shit out.

I still feel bad about it. I don't like hiding things from my dad. Not only is it a lot of work, but it doesn't feel good to keep secrets from someone who has done nothing but love and support me.

Love is an interesting concept in the Selim household. I can count the number of times on one hand that Daddy has said *I love you*—those words, in that order—in my lifetime.

Monique, one of my yoga teachers, says that's an Indian thing. She's also Punjabi and married a guy from Surrey. Small, small world.

"My daughter, Rhekha, says I love you alllll the time to her mataji." *Mataji* means grandmother in Hindi. "Mataji gets so flustered and looks for every available means to exit the conversation at all costs. It's so uncomfortable for her! But that doesn't mean Mataji doesn't *love* Rhekha, it's a matter of expression. Of culture. Some feelings may never be vocalized despite their presence, be it love, hate, hope, fear. It is a flaw of the human condition, but a condition nonetheless."

I didn't understand it until Monique explained it to me like this. I say *I love you* to my mom a lot. To my dad? Zero. Definitely not indicative of his love, the attachment and affection he has for the members of his immediate family (and truly no one else). I don't really understand it, how few people he openly and visibly cares for. Maybe one day I will. Is that a cultural thing, or an Ashar Selim thing? Something to ponder.

I separate hanging out with Tabs, Jonah, and his friends from my respect for my parents. And, let's be real, Mom knows exactly what's up. As always. Sometimes I think I have too many feelings. Heads and hearts harbor histories, especially mine.

My phone bings.

Here 😘

"Call me if you need anything, you know that, Sam."

I nod. "Love you, Mama."

Tabs has been home a week. Her sister walked at graduation. I wrapped up finals. I don't want to overstate how much I studied. In terms of hours? Probably 200 or so. Total. Sounds reasonable to me.

On top of the application workshop for *Harpoon*, I had much on my mind and much to commit to my mind in a very short period of time. Ryan says he understands. His texts keep getting shorter and shorter. (A positive correlation to his patience with me and our relationship?)

Sounds good babe, good luck studying

Keep me posted, you're awesome

You've got this

Great work

Ok

Soon we'll be having emoji-only conversations. The sure signs of a lasting relationship.

I'm glad it's summer. Ryan's now in his fourth year as an ocean lifeguard and gaining seniority. He didn't get Tower 11 as an assignment this season; he says he requested it, but didn't get it added to his schedule.

"They probably had more rookies than normal," he rationalizes.

It's morning, and we're walking from the Blackie's (the surf spot, not the bar) towards his car in the parking lot. "So the department had to give the less busy/fewer rescue towers to them."

"But you got G Street."

G Street is also a less busy/fewer rescue tower.

"Are you saying you think I didn't ask for Tower 11?"

I say no such thing.

"I didn't say that. I'm saying that logic also applies to G Street. So I'm just trying to understand the difference."

"Honestly Sam, I don't make the schedule. If you want to take it up with the captain, be my guest."

Okay bro, what's with the attitude?

"I'll submit my complaint right away. Thank you for your service."

Up ahead maybe ten feet, Ryan's white pickup truck shakes vehemently, like it's offroading in place. A rocket ready to launch. Not a normal scene for a pier parking lot in Newport.

Inside the front seats are two dudes around our age, jamming to their hearts' content, heads banging to the beat of AC/DC's "Shook Me All Night Long."

Hahahahahah. The irony is not lost on me.

The Maloney brothers. I should've known.

The younger one, Ron, wrote, "*I hope you have many years to come with Ryan. Your hot*" in my yearbook last year. Chase is Ryan's age. They've known each other for years. I forget how they met exactly. Maybe at church.

Ryan's pretty religious. His parents are Oklahoma-bred Catholics. My dad was raised Muslim, and my mom, Lutheran. Religions are stories with moral lessons. My parents have instilled a powerful moral code in each of us kids. The narrative varies from religion to religion, from family to family, but ultimately, if you're a good person, you find ways to get along with other good people who share your vision.

Ry uses words like *God, Him, faith, Lord*, etc. pretty often. Not so much with me, but in conversations that include others who share this proclivity, like his church friends and family. I admit, sometimes it makes me uncomfortable. Not in an *I detest religion* kind of way, just in the way that it's unfamiliar. In the *what we don't know scares us* kind of way. The more he talks about his faith, the more I learn and appreciate his heart for the church. And the more this part of his life becomes more familiar. And less scary.

'Cause the walls start shaking . . .

My head bobs from right to left in tune with the melody. Then my shoulders. Then my hips. That's what you get for telling your bros where you keep your car keys while you're in the water. While creative, the tailpipe is not exactly secure.

Ryan all but throws his shortboard into the truck bed before yanking fruitlessly on the driver's side door.

The doors are locked.

To the average observer, his grinning mug indicates permissioned participation in the joke. But I can tell he's peeved. He wouldn't make a scene in front of the boys. He'll probably tell them I have to be home soon and needs to hurry up and get changed.

"You dudes are such kooks." Tight with rage, his voice sounds dry like unbuttered toast. "I gotta get Sam home soon, can you open the door?"

Called that. Perhaps he forgot I rode my bike today?

I clearly still haven't gotten used to it. One of the things I don't like about Ryan is his need to appear in control when it comes to me.

"Maybe it's time to find a new hiding place for your keys." My attempt at distracting myself from his naivete is all but futile. "Perhaps you might consider above the wheel?"

"Don't be a smartass, Sam, I'm not in the mood for your sass."

Enough is enough.

"Maybe I'm not in the mood for your petulance." I turn on my bare heel and make my way towards Charlie's Chili, where my bike is parked. I don't look back.

He doesn't come after me. By then Chase and Ron are out of the car and on their way to shower off the saltwater and sand. Which they obviously tracked into Ryan's car. He calls me from his phone, once, twice. He sends a text:

*Sorry I didn't mean it. I'm just
stressed. Plz come back*

My combination lock clicks open. I collect the chord and mount the cruiser. He sees me from one hundred feet away. I doubt he sees my expression.

Because I'm crying, softly, to myself. I'm wearing my green-flash Ray Bans, so no one can see my swollen eyelids.

It's almost 9 a.m. I'll see Tabs soon. And I'll forget about this forgettable morning.

Except for the car jacking. That was just hilarious.

Chapter 48

When I get home, I park my bike next to the garage to save time so I don't have to pull it out again when Tabs arrives. I tie it to the railing by the stairs leading up to the back patio. A.K.A., Mama's Jungle.

In the ten minutes it takes me to ride from the pier to the house, my tears have dried, but the stains have left some indelible pink marks in the corners of my eyes. I'll just put on a healthy helping of eye liner. No one will know the difference.

I change out of my matching Z Supply sweats and hoodie, opting for my black Skatie bikini, cut-offs, and white tank top. I toss my kashmari shawl—turquoise and bedazzled—into my Apolis tote, embossed with *Lido Isle, California* on it.

(The Apolis brand supports Bangledeshi women in earning fair wages and having access to health insurance. These bags are the same kind of market bags made in the 1970s after Bangladesh's independence, after first becoming East Pakistan following partition from India in the 1940s. Notable history lesson for a great cause. Plus, it reminds me of the kind man I met on my flight to England.)

My phone has been buzzing every few minutes.

Talk to me please

I love you

Don't be mad

I've lost my patience. I don't even know if it's patience. Respect? Interest? All of the above?

Perhaps I've reached my boiling point. Or is it tipping point? I think both might apply here.

At this point last year, I would've stewed for a few hours, called him, during which time we would emote (both of us) for hours, make up, and move on.

Today, though, is different. Today, I know more about him, and honestly, and more importantly, more about me. My BS threshold is a lot lower than it used to be.

Eventually, after about an hour, the texts are fewer and far between. Until they stop altogether. Tabs hears the buzzing through the burlap fabric of my tote. She doesn't say anything about it.

Until . . .

"How are things with Ryan?" We're barely out of the alley and onto the boardwalk as we head towards the Fun Zone to lock up our bikes.

It's unlike me to not answer, so I manage a "Good," followed immediately by, "what's the plan?"

She takes the hint (bless her heart) and smiles devilishly.

"Jonah and Turbo are picking us up on the other side of the ferry on the island. We'll go to Turbo's house in Newport Coast to hang by the pool for a while. That's as far as we got."

By "we", she means her and Jonah. She's only been home a week and they've managed to see each other pretty much every day since. They're so cute together. So happy.

Ryan and I were happy once. Until we weren't.

Boarding the ferry on the peninsula side, Tabs and I ride the cross-harbor vessel to Balboa Island. I loved the ferry when I was a kid. In fact, I loved it so much that my dad would take me on rides just riding back and forth so I could watch the sea lions pop up next to the side of the boat. I'd point and squeal in delight. We went back and forth so much the ferry captain stopped collecting ferry fare. Can you believe it was fifty cents to ride the ferry back then?

As we got older, i.e. learned to ride bikes, we'd take the ferry to the island on Sundays. We'd ride up Jamboree towards the Back Bay, now a natural preserve of sorts for marine and wildlife. I believe it's called an estuary, a mix of fresh and saltwater.

My favorite part was on the way back, when we'd stop at Dad's to get hippo cookies. They're just what they sound like: cookies in the shape of hippos, with M&Ms for eyes and sprinkles on the butt. I still go get them sometimes.

The boys arrive a few minutes late, true to form. What's with boys and punctuality? Or lack thereof?

"The drive-thru line at In-n-Out was really long." Turbo greets us with a disarming smile through his rolled-down window. "So we got you burgers and shakes to make up for it," Jonah adds as he exits the back seat and kisses Tabs on the cheek.

"You're forgiven," I chirp as I snag what I presume to be my vanilla milkshake and settle into the front seat. Tabs and Jonah need their privacy. "So, where we going?"

"A chick who gets to the point! I dig it." Turbo reverses his clydesdale of a whip and turns onto Agate Ave. Many of the streets on the island are named for precious gemstones, like topaz and garnet. The Grand Canal splits Little Balboa Island from the larger part of the island. For comparison, it's definitely not as grand as the one in Venice of the same name. Same spirit, though. It's got a car and foot bridge connecting both sides.

"Easy bro, she's taken." Jonah reminds Turbo he needs to respect the boundary.

"Lucky guy, that Ryan."

Getting back to the point, "Meaning we're on our way toooooo . . ." My *ooooo* implies a fill-in-the-blank.

"Right, right, we're heading towards my place in Newport Coast. Plan is to hang by the pool and see where the day takes us. Cool?"

"Cool."

Newport Coast, the city's most recent addition, sits behind Crystal Cove State Park, a left turn off PCH as you're heading south towards Laguna. An Irvine Company gem, it includes Pelican Hill and its renowned golf course. The Newport Coast arch, visible from PCH, is something of an icon.

After cruising through Corona del Mar on PCH, we end up at the community pool maybe twenty minutes later.

Community pool doesn't do this place justice. It's more like a resort spa, sans the services. But the amenities—pool, jacuzzi, sauna—are similar. Except there is a towel service. Self-serve, but still.

The cabanas hang like canopies over the north side of the space, across from the entrance. Daybeds, white with cushioned bodies, extend beyond the edge of the shade. Such is noontime in late June. I love the sun. I haven't worn sunscreen basically ever, a testament to the melanin from my dad. I get really dark in the summer. My skin is basically seasonal. In India, dark skin is considered a sign of poverty. In fact, some cultures encourage bleaching to appear more fair, more white. Which is interesting, because sunless tanning products account for over a billion dollars of the US beauty market.

The world can be a strange, inconsistent place.

While Tabs and Jonah canoodle on a daybed, I find a spot in the sun next to the shallow end of the pool. Easy access for dips. And it's safer. Mama would be so proud. I know my limits.

There's no one here besides a young dad and his son, wading around in the kiddie pool behind the grills. They leave eventually, after the two-year-old throws a fit and begs for his mama.

After a brief vaping session (I can only assume), Turbo joins me on the steps of the shallow end of the pool.

"How's the boyfriend?"

"Good."

"Good? Uh-oh. Trouble in paradise?"

"What makes you say that?"

"The shorter the answer, the more trouble there is. It's an inverse relationship. I think that's what it's called? I didn't do so great in trig. B minus."

He stifles a laugh before claiming silence, probably meant for me to fill with my less-than-convincing explanation. If you could even call it that. An explanation? Rationalization? Defense?

"Plus, your phone won't stop buzzing. You're beautiful and all, but you hardly seem like the type to spread yourself around like that." The calls started again once we arrived at the pool.

"What makes you say that?" I sound like a parrot. I should probably turn off my phone. Or block him.

"You've got this quiet innocence about you. Not prude, just, more selective."

"Thanks, I guess. I can't tell if that's a compliment or not."

"It is, absolutely. You really don't know how beautiful you are. I can tell just by talking to you."

He's right. I've never thought of myself as beautiful. I think of myself as smart, curious, resourceful even. But never beautiful. I think of my insides more than my outsides. Maybe that's a guy thing? To notice the physical stuff first? Dustin told me once that he prefers to sleep with a girl first before he invests any time in getting to know her. He made it sound like a typical guy thing to do.

"Because if the sex is bad the relationship is a waste of time." No wonder we stopped talking. I obviously wasn't going to sleep with him. It all makes sense.

Biologically, men pursue women they're physically attracted to first, then they figure out if they like their minds, if that plays a factor at all. It's all about passing on their genes. That's the science of it. Modern America forgets to mention that in this tech-driven world. I wouldn't be surprised if my posterity is part cyborg.

He's studying me as I'm falling down the rabbit hole of my own mind. I pretend not to notice.

"You're going to break up with him, aren't you." It's a statement, not a question.

Before I can formulate a clever response, Jonah saunters over, probably to make sure Turbo is behaving himself.

"Just wanted to make sure Turbo is behaving himself."

Uh-huh.

"He's walking the line, but I'm keeping him in his place."

"Did you just slide a Johnny Cash reference into a conversation about how I'm not hitting on you?"

"Maybe."

"I just fell in love."

Jonah splashes Turbo. Actually, it's more of a mini tsunami that gathers its momentum from the four-foot depth of the pool. They start wrestling in the water, something of an agro version of synchronized swimming.

That's my cue to join Tabs, allow the boys some time to release their testosterone on each other.

"Having fun?" She's applying the most amazing smelling sunscreen as I walk up to her from the opposite end of the pool.

"You know I love a good show." I nod towards the boys getting rowdy.

"Yeah, they're cute though. At least you have a brother, you know how they are."

"My brother is eleven. Aside from the competition thing, I've got zero insights on teen boys."

"You have Ryan."

"Ryan doesn't count. He's an enigma."

"How so?"

Where do I begin?

"First of all, he cries. All. The. Time."

She laughs.

"I'm serious! Honestly, I like that he cries. Men should be encouraged to cry. It's healthier than penting up all that emotion inside and releasing it as anger. But Ryan? He's sooooo sensitive. I mean, I know I'm sensitive. But he takes it to another level. The reason he cries most times is because he's *disappointing* me. What does that even mean?"

"He probably thinks you're too good for him. And he's scared of disappointing you. His insecurities are taking over, and he probably doesn't even realize it."

How did she do that? Just like, say it so matter-of-factly?

"He doesn't realize it . . . " I let my words linger a bit, so I can feel their weight on my tongue.

She's right. He doesn't. In all the conversations we've had on the subject, he just wants everything to be okay, for me to forgive him, so we can move on. I believe in that, moving on, but not if there aren't efforts made to fix the issues, so they don't repeat. Otherwise history repeats itself.

Should it be my job to make him feel more secure? Absolutely not. That's an inside job.

"Sam?"

I zone out for a few minutes before I realize Tabs is tapping me on the shoulder.

"Sorry."

"Another rabbit hole?" She can't hide her smirk.

"The deepest one yet."

By the time the boys satiate their competitive urges, it's almost two o'clock.

"Hungry?" Turbo smacks his lips while drying himself off with the blue and white striped towel.

"Didn't we just have lunch?"

"That was hours ago! I'm a growing boy! I need my fuel!" Stroking his belly, or rather, his six-pack, Turbo emphasizes his need for sustenance.

"Let's grub at Wahoo's. I'm craving a steak quesadilla. Ladies? Thoughts?"

It's true. When you drive as a teenager, food is the number one destination.

Wahoo's is a fast-casual, mostly Mexican restaurant that was started by the Lee family in Costa Mesa in the late 80s. Flavors include influences from Brazil and Asia, like their cajun fries and kalua pig bowl. I'm a fan of the mahi burrito myself.

We make it over to the restaurant in about half an hour. Located in the atrium food court in Fashion Island, we hit the lull between lunch and dinner.

"You got a nice glow today, Sam," Jonah comments on my new shades of brown. "You must be at least a hundred shades darker than Ryan."

"Probably."

"What's he up to today?"

"I'm not sure, actually." I bite into my burrito with intention. "I saw him this morning after his surf."

"No date night plans?"

"No, not tonight."

"But it's a summer Saturday!"

"JONAH, leave her alone." Tabs to the rescue.

"What? I was just asking—"

"It's okay. I'll be right back, I need to use the restroom." I know she'll fill him in while I'm gone. Better her than me.

I take my phone with me. He hasn't tried to get ahold of me for a while. Like a couple hours or so. Do I open the can of worms and make the call?

Not right now.

I text him instead:

> *Hey, I'm with Tabs. can we talk tomorrow in person?*

Merely seconds go by before he responds with:

> *Of course. Morning work? I can come to you*

How accommodating.

*That would be great. 9am ok? 7th
street?*

I need physical distance from our memories for this conversation.

*7th street it is. See you then. I love
you Samantha*

He never uses my given name.

He knows what's coming.

Chapter 49

"Seventh street. We've never had a rendezvous here before."

One of the things I don't like about Ryan is how oblivious he can be sometimes.

I didn't sleep last night. Every time I looked at the clock, barely a few minutes had passed. And that was every few minutes.

I told Tabs my plan, about seeing Ryan this morning. What I wanted to say.

"I think you're being very brave. It's hard, when you know you're going to hurt someone you love. Only he can control how he reacts. I hope he proves he's a good guy."

"Yeah, I figured it'd be a change of scenery for us.

"Look, Sam, I'm really sorry about yester—"

"Can I go first? Before we get to the apology portion of the program, I'd like to say a few things."

"Um, okay."

He totally knows.

"You know I love you. It's not about that. Lately, I've noticed we haven't been getting along. Maybe that's not the right way to describe it. I mean . . ."

Searching, searching here . . .

"I mean we've been finding reasons to pick each other apart. And it's not only not fun, it's exhausting. I'm physically tired from it all. I'm sixteen, I shouldn't be tired. I'm not going through menopause."

We're standing a few feet apart. I'm looking him in the eye, or trying to at least. He's looking at his feet.

I continue. "I don't think it's either of our faults. I think, maybe, we've just outgrown each other. Maybe, we need different things. And maybe, those things, we can't give to each other. Maybe we need to get them from somewhere else. Does that make sense?"

I'm losing him. It's all over his face, in his shuffling, in his pockets where he's hiding his hands.

"So, it's over?" A question, not a statement.

"I think it is."

A few moments settle in between us, bridging the reality of being together, then not.

"Is there anything I can say to change your mind?"

Groveling. How becoming.

"I don't think so. No."

No. N. O.

"Did I not love you enough? I can be better, babe, really. I want to be better for you. I've never loved anyone like I've loved you. I thought I was going to marry you."

Oh dear, I've lost him.

"You didn't hear a word I just said, did you?"

Silence pervades, aside from bikes and pedestrians wisping behind us on the boardwalk a few yards away.

"These things you need, what are they?"

Yikes. On the spot.

"I don't know, Ry. I don't want to drag you along with me while I figure it out. That's not fair to you."

"What if I want to be dragged along?"

This is getting more depressing by the minute.

"Why would you possibly want that?"

"Because it means I would get more time with you."

Sorry I asked. Apparently the delicate approach solves nothing.

"I love you, Ryan, but we're done. We're young—maybe in another time, when we've had some time apart, we can try again."

Hope, he needs hope right now.

"You mean that?"

I consider it.

"Yes. I do."

His arms embrace me, the beariest of bear hugs. He smells like the sea, mixed with the Agua D'Eau I love so much.

"And we can still be friends? Like, I can call you to talk and for advice and stuff?"

This is the breakup that wouldn't end.

"Sure, still friends. It would suck if we couldn't still be friends."

And I was doing so well.

"Good. As friends, are you free for dinner tonight?"

Holy hell. Help me.

"Actually, I can't. I have plans."

"With who?" He looks like a sad puppy.

None of your damn business.

"Tabs."

"Didn't you just see her last night?"

My eyes bore into his forehead. He has three heads and a horn coming out of his nose, as far as I'm concerned.

"Sorry, I don't have the right to ask that anymore."

You never had the right to ask that.

"I should be getting home. I told my dad I was going for a run, that was an hour ago." We've been teetering on the brink of infinity for longer than is probably acceptable for a normal breakup. I don't know for sure, since this is my first one. But I'm willing to put money on it.

"Right, okay. Let me walk you back."

"Oh, um. Okay."

"What's wrong?" He senses my hesitation.

"Well, I was thinking I'd actually go on a run, before I go home."

He's sad.

"It would look suspicious if I went home now and wasn't sweating."

Always three steps behind, this one.

"Good thinking. See, you're always three steps ahead of me."

At least he's not wrong. Just not as quick.

"We'll talk later." I gather some breath. "Just so you know, this was hard for me, too."

Before he can reply, I peck him on the cheek and start my run towards the Wedge.

I swear I taste salt.

After filling Mama in, Tabs is my first call.

"You're a free woman!" she chants more gleefully than I would have expected. "Tonight is going to be SO fun. Jonah's friend Kane is coming, and he totallllllly adores you."

"Tabs, I've been single for ten minutes. Go easy on me, will you? It was hard. And I feel like shit."

I do, though, feel like shit. I may have broken his heart, but I also broke mine in the process. It's not irreparable, this heart of mine. I do need the space, the time. Sometimes things fall apart, so better things can fall together. I must've read that on an IG post somewhere.

"I get it, girl. Feel the feelings. But I also think a distraction wouldn't be the worst thing."

She's probably right. Knowing me, my rabbit hole will be wider and deeper than ever, and I don't need that kind of drama—no matter how self-inflicted the source of the drama. Focus on what you can control.

"Yeah, okay," I hear myself concede. "Where are we going, and what do I need to tell my parents?"

The plan turns into Jonah, Turbo, Rick, and Kane meeting for dinner at Ruby's on the pier. The symbolism strikes me in the gut, hard, like a spear searing a wicked tuna. Where the beginning and the end commingle.

Mom agrees to drop Tabs off at home no later than 10:30 p.m. Meaning, Mom will pick us up from wherever we end up by 10.

"As long as it's within Newport's city limits." Fair.

We're meeting the guys at 6. Tabs is getting dropped off around 5:30.

The big question is, what should I wear?

Chapter 50

I opt for a long, chiffon black maxi dress from Common Thread that ties in the back. The straps are slinky, nearly the thickness of spooling thread. The front covers all it needs to; the dress's shape billows around my hips, hiding the narrowness of my waist and the fullness of my hips. IYKYK.

I recently bought this rose gold ear cuff. The piece of jewelry wraps around the thickest part of the cartilage in an "X" design. It makes me look a little edgy. My ears aren't pierced—I've had them pierced twice in my young life already. Once, when I was about two years old, and again when I was in third grade. Apparently I'm not responsible enough for ear care. Both times the ear holes closed up. I do have thick earlobes, so my ears in all their glory are predisposed to closure—even though I did wait the recommended four to six weeks after piercing until I removed the studs.

My hair touches the middle of my back now. I haven't cut it, like *really* cut it, in a couple of years now. I go to Christine for regular trims every couple of months, but that's it. I've grown out my side-swept bangs too. Too much hassle to maintain. As someone who doesn't spend a whole lot of time in front of the mirror—at least, compared to other teenage girls—I just don't have the patience to devote that kind of time to something like hair. A few brush strokes and we're in business.

Jonah is right. My skin exudes a warm, healthy glow. In the winter, I'm still darker than my classmates, just more olive in tone. My skin, like the seasons, rotates along with the Earth.

Tabs arrives promptly at 5:30 p.m. By six, we're walking up the ramp between Tower A and Tower M towards the restaurant at the end of the pier. Against reasonable expectation, the boys already have a table.

Walking in, we see them sitting in a corner booth nestled against the window, with views of the horizon. There's a seat open next to Rick and Kane. I presume it's for me. Jonah sits across from them, holding an open chair for Tabs.

"Think they planned to get here early to pick their seats?" Tabs whispers as we walk in, though it's not quite a whisper.

The things boys think to be strategic about.

We have a nice meal. I order the bleus burger, fries, and an Oreo Cookie shake. I deserve it, after the weekend I've had.

"You can eat! I like that." Kane intends his observation to be a compliment. I can tell by his gentle smile. Ugh, those dimples.

Afterwards, we decide to head over to Kane's so we can see his guitar collection. Sounds cool, I guess. I'm open to expanding my knowledge about bass and other strings. Rick drives us over.

Kane lives in Cameo Shores. Opposite Cameo Highlands, this neighborhood abuts the coastline just before El Morro and Laguna. There are so many little villages across Newport, I discover a new one every time I make a new acquaintance. And I've lived here my whole life!

His home is a Spanish pueblo, on steroids. A courtyard anchors the building, complete with a salt water pool and jacuzzi. The east wing (literally, a wing) houses the four bedrooms, including a master bedroom with the highest ceilings I've ever seen. The west wing consists of the primary entertainment spaces: living room, adjoining chef's kitchen, family room, and wine cellar. The open concept connects the spaces so that they don't feel like separate rooms, but one flowing room hosting different experiences depending on the mood and occasion.

"His dad is an heir to a vineyard in South America," Tabs answers the *who is responsible for all this wealth* question.

"Brazilian bush babies," Jonah offers up his interpretation of the situation.

Kane's guitars live in a separate corner of the house, in the east wing, past the bedrooms and attached to the pool house. He has every model ever created, from Fenders (a Stratocaster and Telecaster) to Gibsons (a Les Paul and SG). Or so I'm learning. My mom has a Gibson. She's the most musical member of the family. She plays piano regularly. She taught me through two levels of instruction once. I can play "Ode to Joy" by memory. Reading notes doesn't come naturally to me like it does to her. Or maybe it's just another indication of our distance on the spectrum of patience. Honestly, it's probably more the latter.

"Do you play?" Kane picks up a remarkable-looking Gibson, crisp, bleached wood resembling a dance floor fit for the principal dancers of American Ballet Theatre.

"If by play, you mean the game of life? Hell yeah. Guitars? Not so much."

He laughs, genuinely.

"You're funny, Samantha. Funnier than I expected."

Thank you? Backhanded compliments are all the rage this weekend. When it rains, it pours, hails, and white-outs.

I'm more captivated by the decor of the room. Black wallpaper with subtle silver herringbone accents bounce light from an industrial chandelier in the center of the ceiling. Glass cases house the art, the guitars, in a neat arrangement, using a logic unknown to me but seemingly sensical.

"Can I play you a song?"

This guy will not lay off.

"Sure."

"Do you like *Bohemian Rhapsody*?"

"Yes! Oh yes!" Tabs loves Queen. And Freddie. Gosh, even Adam Lambert. "My heroes!" She recognizes her role in the cock block immediately. "Obviously, Sam's answer is more important than mine." She grabs Jonah's hand and escapes to the pool area, where Rick is taking a nap. At least, he looks like he's taking a nap.

Which leaves Kane and me all by our lonesomes.

"As a matter of fact, I do like *Bohemian Rhapsody*."

He plays an acoustic version. It's soulful and effusive and core-shaking. I'm on the brink of tears suddenly. I take deep breaths through my nose, hoping my nerves will get ahold of themselves.

They do not.

"I need to use the restroom. Can you tell me where it is?"

Concern washes over his face. "Second door on the right." He points down the hallway paved with family portraits, mostly of international travel. "You okay?"

"I'm fine, I think I just have sand in my eyes." When in doubt, blame the beach.

Turquoise tiles of various shades line the vanity. Abalone accents border the wash bowl, shining luminescent from the uplighting within the countertop. Easily the most beautiful bathroom I've ever seen.

I'm hiding here. That's my intention until I can pull it together. There's a stool next to the vanity—turquoise fabric and white legs— I plop onto while I sort through my feelings.

Why am I even sad? *Duh, Sam, you just ended a relationship with a person you love. Obviously you're sad. Shake it off. Taylor would want you to.*

I collect myself over a few more breaths. Good thing I don't wear a ton of eye makeup. I'd look like one of those mod mime actors by now.

I haven't been gone long, maybe ten minutes. Kane is messing around with a few chords when I get back.

"You okay?" He sounds a little confused. Boys can be so dumb.

"Yeah, I'm good. What else can you play?"

He smiles, grateful for the opportunity to show off his skills.

For the next ten or twenty minutes, I'm half-listening to the strum of the harmony from "I Want To Break Free" while making beleaguered attempts to calm my racing heart.

Breakups are really stressful all around, aren't they. (A statement, not a question.)

Tabs meanders back into the room, probably to check on me. She says it's a full moon tonight and wants to head to Lookout Point to check it out.

"I dig a good moon sighting. Sam, you down?" Kane looks at me for affirmation, while Tabs walks over to my left and grabs my hand without a word.

"Yeah, I'm in." Three syllables never took so much effort.

"Don't worry, you're doing great. Kane really likes you."

"How can you tell?" I'm really too obvious about such things. If history is any indication.

"For one thing, he can't stop staring at you." That's true, I guess. "Plus, he told Jonah he can't believe how beautiful and smart you are."

"Oh." I don't know what else to say. My brain is playing catch up with my voice.

We pile back into Rick's Honda CRV and make our way towards Lookout Point. This time, Tabs takes the front seat. I'm sandwiched between Kane and Jonah in the back. Not exactly romantic, but I appreciate the attempt at encouraging some proximity for Kane and me. There's some definite knee-knocking and shoulder rubbing. Contact is contact.

Lookout Point sits atop the cliffs of Corona del Mar, specifically above the channel entrance that feeds into Newport Harbor. My parents almost bought a home up there, near the point, when they were looking for houses before they got married. They got so far as bankruptcy court, because the owners had run out of money while renovating the place. They had a firm stance on their budget. Instead, they bought our house, which I prefer. Up there, the beach seems so far away. But I guess I'm biased.

But the view really is spectacular. You can see the Wedge across the way, one of the biggest, baddest waves in the world. And Catalina beyond it, and Laguna and its coastal inlets to the south. There's a park where you can picnic and chill. Or get stoned and drunk, if you're into that.

The sunset is viewable at most times of year from here. Down by where we are, it's harder to see in the summer, because west is slightly behind the rooftops. But the moon. The moon is different. Tonight it looks like it's pinned just above the tallest palm tree nearby. It glows a pearly white, with hints of yellow, like it's tainted or something. But it's complete. Even when it's not full, it's still whole. I love that.

It's after eight and just barely past sunset. We park down Heliotrope and walk the half block towards the greenbelt. Tabs and Jonah lead the way, followed by Rick, then Kane and me. We're chatting comfortably. My confidence is intact. I even nudge him a little.

Hey, look at me, I'm flirting! We can thank Tabs for that. Sometimes you just need a reminder.

I think I feel my phone buzz, but I ignore it for now. I'll check it later. My flow shall not be interrupted.

I feel it again, and again, and again.

No.

It can't be.

My screen shows six missed calls. Apparently, Ryan has decided he needs to reach me THIS MINUTE.

WTF.

I put the phone back in my purse and continue my banter with Kane.

"My tongue is very flexible." I don't know how we got there, but here we are. I think that means he wants to kiss me.

"It's one of the most athletic muscles in the body." Obviously, I'd be the one to insert a fun fact in an otherwise borderline raunchy conversation.

"But mine," Kane continues, "mine gives gymnasts a run for their money."

The vibrations continue. I'm hoping they're phantoms, but Kane hears them too.

"Do you need to get that?" Our flow is interrupted.

"No. No, I don't."

I take his hand and slide it into mine. Not a perfect fit, but it will do. His intently focused eyes indicate he's okay with it.

We're wandering the perimeter of the park. Tabs and Jonah find a seat on a bench and proceed to make out. Rick . . . Well, I don't know where Rick is.

Kane and I are moving away from the park now, down the stairs towards Pirate's Cove. He's leading me, turning behind every few steps to steady me, as the steps are pretty steep. His right hand grazes my hips gently. He looks at me for consent. I give it to him.

The vibrations linger like poorly selected background music.

He pretends not to notice now. Or manages to tune them out. I can't tell.

They're like a chau gong gone rogue in my own ears.

We make it down the stairs and find a seat on top on the cove. Our feet dangle over the opening thirty feet above the beach. It feels risky, but I like it.

My body temperature drops as the minutes pass. Kane peels off his Northface zip-up and wraps it around my shoulders without a word.

I reach into my purse and mute the sound. I probably should have done that a while ago.

Eighteen missed calls and seven text messages.

"You're so popular." Kane turns towards me. We're close, sitting maybe three inches apart.

"You're teasing me, aren't you?" I playfully throw my left shoulder so that it skims his right one. The momentum scoots my butt towards him so that three inches is now no inches.

"Maybe. But you can handle it." His right hand now rests on my left thigh.

I don't know what to say next. So, I just breathe. I breathe in the moment, the smell of Kane's cologne, the salty air.

"I'd really like to kiss you." Direct. "Would that be okay?" His left hand finds its way to my right cheek, so that all I can see are the whites of his eyes in the darkness.

"Yes." It's more of a croak than a word, but he heard me just fine.

It's surprisingly not good. I didn't think it was possible. His mouth is closed the whole time, so it feels like I'm kissing my own arm. I use my tongue to pry open his lips, to no avail. At this point I don't think I'll ever know just how flexible his tongue actually is.

Is this payback for not answering any of Ryan's calls? Who knows.

After what feels like forever, I rest my head on his shoulder and pray he got what he wanted.

"You're a great kisser," he pants into my hair. I wonder how many girls he's kissed before?

"Thank you." I offer him a smile as a sign of gratitude. "Maybe we should head back up? It's getting late, and Tabs and I have a curfew to meet."

"Too bad, I was really enjoying myself." He stands first and helps me up. By the time we get back up the hill it's almost nine. Plenty of time to make it back for Mama to pick us up. I have this uncanny sense around time. Like, I always know what time it is, even without my phone. I can't explain it.

I'm afraid to look at how many more missed calls I have from you-know-who. I feel bad ignoring him, really, I do. But calling me incessantly ALL DAY does not make me want to talk to him at all. Like, how needy are you?

But I have to look at my phone to text Mama about our pickup spot: Barnes and Noble at Fashion Island.

Against my better judgement, I call him back, then and there.

"Hey, what's up?"

"Are you okay? I've been calling you all day."

"I can see that. I'm out right now. Is everything okay?"

"Who are you with?" His tone is accusatory, but also sad. Like a vengeful puppy after his bone is taken away.

"Well, Ryan, that's none of your business." At the mention of his name, everyone in the car looks at me. "Do you need something right now?"

"Why won't you tell me?"

"Is that why you've been calling me all day? To ask me who I'm hanging out with?"

He responds with silence, followed by a few gulps of breath. He's whimpering now.

"This is really unfair of you, Ryan. I don't have anything to say. Have a good night." And with that I end the conversation. It feels shitty. But he needs me to say it. Hasn't he learned anything about boundaries?

"Ryan has been calling you all day?" Jonah doesn't attempt to hide his disbelief.

"I think he's having a hard time." I don't want to shine a bad light, any more than maybe already has been.

"Well, he should suck it up and leave you alone. He's not your problem anymore."

I don't think Jonah means it the way it comes out. Maybe he does.

I never viewed Ryan as my problem. I don't think. Something about that comment sticks with me.

Kane kisses me on the cheek outside the car in the parking lot at BN. "I'd like to ask you for your phone number, but I'm not sure it's such a good idea . . ."

I appreciate his candor. "You can get it from Jonah." Somehow that feels less douchey than giving it to him myself, considering I broke up with my boyfriend, who is clearly not handling it well, hours ago.

"Deal."

Tabs loops her arm through mine. "Good night boys, we'll talk to you later."

She steers me in the direction of the bookstore's entrance. I see Mom's car turning right from Jamboree towards us. Right on time.

"Do you need to talk?" Tabs rubs my arm, soothing and maternal as she is.

"I just want the day to be over."

Chapter 51

"I don't even know what to call it." I'm chatting with Mama over coffee and sourdough toast in the kitchen the next morning. "It's like he had a total meltdown."

Mama sips her half-hazelnut, half-vanilla blend mixed with milk and sugar. The *Wall Street Journal* lays open to the Lifestyle section on her personal bistro table. Today there's an article about tropical plants. Her specialty.

I sit on one of the bar stools next to the island, facing her seat by the window that looks out into her garden. We spend a lot of time in this spot, her and I.

"Well, honey," she muses between sips, "he's probably really hurting. And just doesn't know how to handle it. You mean a lot to him."

"But that shouldn't excuse his behavior! It was totally unacceptable. Like, I was embarrassed for him."

""No, no, it's not an excuse. But maybe cut him some slack? This might be the first time he's ever felt like this." She takes a bite of her toast and chews.

"But is it my responsibility to make sure he handles it? I don't think so."

"Sammy." She's getting serious now. I can hear it in her tone. "Whether you like it or not, you play that role for people. It's who you are. How many times have your friends called you for advice?" I think about it. Back to the time I used to have friends. "You are that source of perspective for them. It's one of your strengths."

She's not wrong. I guess I never thought of it like that. She hasn't even seen the volume of texts that fall under this category. She's good.

"So do I treat Ryan like normal, like everything's okay? What if he can't separate our friendship from our . . . relationship?"

"Give him some time. It'll take a while to adjust, for both of you." I haven't told her about my own milder version of a meltdown in Kane's bathroom. "You know how impatient you can be."

Yeah, yeah, I know.

"I guess I'm just worried that he'll continue to be this super clingy person in my life, and that we'll never move forward."

"Sammy, honey, don't worry about it until it becomes a problem."

I smirk at her. She knows that's one of my -isms, my life mottos.

"Now, I was thinking about going shopping today. There's a really cute skirt at Havana Banana I want to get for Hawaii."

I can't resist an outburst of laughter, followed by a few snickers. "You mean, Tommy Bahama?" Sometimes I'm literally the only person who can interpret her misspeakings. It's part of our special bond.

"Yeah, that!" She holds up her coffee mug, which is decorated with a *Cheers* tribute to the Boston bar of the same name, in salute.

"Okay, shopping sounds like fun. What time you thinking? Eleven or so?" Mama doesn't leave the house before then, unless she's taking us to school. It's around nine right now.

"Sounds good to me!"

I think I'll write in my journal for a little while before I get ready. Writing helps me clear my thoughts, sort out my feelings, that kind of thing. Maybe I'll write a letter to Ryan? Say all I need to say. Then figure out what to share later, when we talk? Because, after talking to Mama, it's the right thing to do.

I think.

Chapter 52

Dear Ryan,

I'm not really sure where to begin. Yesterday was rough, for a lot of reasons. In the morning, especially, when we decided to end our romantic relationship. It was one of the most difficult conversations I've ever had. You should know that. When you start a new relationship, you don't think of what the ending will look like. At least, I didn't think that way. You were my first boyfriend. And you were a _great_ first boyfriend. I learned so much from you, about myself and the person I want to be. I also learned who I don't want to be, which is equally if not more important. Why? Because light cannot exist without shadow. Both are necessary to existence. So, while scary, learning about the shadow part of me is probably one of the most valuable lessons I learned from being your girlfriend.

You're probably wondering what the shadow part is. (Because obviously, the light is much more apparent. It's the nurturing part, the motivating part, the supportive, follow your dreams, part.) The shadow part is less uplifting, more sunkening, if that's a word. I learned that, for me, it's the part of me that craves exploration, at any cost. Well, maybe not any cost, but to a point where I'm focused on myself and not anyone else. Including those I love. You know how I always talk about boundaries? Well, I realize mine are not as defined as I may have thought before. While I believe boundaries evolve, as they do with borders and city lines, I need to be more definitive of what mine are when it comes to people and my own happiness. Bob Marley says everyone will hurt you, you just have to figure out who's worth suffering for, or something like that. And I believe that. I'm too stubborn today to not have what I believe I deserve. Who knows if that will change twenty, thirty years from now. But that's my truth today, so that's what I'm going off of.

I need to say that the way you called me incessantly all day yesterday was not okay. Not just because it was a pain in the ass for me, but it's not a helpful exercise for you. What did you want to accomplish? What did you want your outcome to be? To be honest, I'm not sure you even know. And that's okay. But I want to be clear here that I can't be constantly available to you, even as a friend. You need to find some confidence in yourself, to deal with your own life. I know you're a confident person, we wouldn't have been together if you weren't. So, I ask you to figure out why you did that—call and text me for an entire day— and what you thought you'd get out of it. I really don't think it has anything to do with me, personally. I don't say that to avoid responsibility. I say it because you're looking for something that I can't give you. And it's up to you to figure out what that is.

This might be a bad thing to say right now, but I do love you. I think you have so much to offer. But just like you have things to work on, I have things to work on too. And at this point, I owe it to myself to be selfish and figure out my way through it. I meant it when I said I wanted to be friends. But maybe for now, we need some time apart, to become the next iteration of ourselves, individual and independent. I hope you're okay with that. Because that's what I need. And I suspect that is what you need too.

And for what it's worth, we'll always have Tower 11.

-Sammy

Chapter 53

Mama and I spend the day shopping at Tommy Bahama, in the shopping center off PCH and MacArthur with the Jack's Surfboards and Sprinkles Cupcake Bakery in it. She *loves* anything related to Hawaii: clothes, food, knickknacks.

This summer, we're going to Maui for ten days in August. We try to go every other year, because Mom loves it so much. She says she fell in love with it after Jim, her first husband, died; she went there to get away and mourn, really, following his accident. Daddy doesn't like Hawaii. It's too humid for him. So it's just Mama and the kids. I think it's a nice vacation for my dad, too.

He's recovering well from his surgery earlier this year. He doesn't take as many morning walks as he once did; he doesn't cover as much ground, either. At his healthiest, he would run to Huntington Beach, which is about fifteen miles round trip. But he gets outside and enjoys the salty sea air. Time changes us, and in some cases, slows us down. It draws wrinkles and weakens bones.

It's hard to watch my dad get older, more fragile. Despite this, to me, he will always be strong.

I find this great blue-patterned skirt. It has palm trees on it set against a setting sun. Mama buys it for me. "You've had an eventful weekend. Consider it a life event gift."

The life event—ending my first "serious" relationship with the first boy I ever loved. Yes, I would definitely call that a life event.

I wait a few days to send Ryan my letter. I noodle hard on whether to send him the whole thing, parts of it, or write something completely different. I have to type it out anyway, since the original is handwritten in my personal journal. I guess I could take a photo of it and send it like that, but that just seems lazy. I'm not lazy.

Ultimately, I decide to share it as-is, typed out. Pure and raw, just like our relationship was. It will change. I know this. How, is the question. But only time will tell.

Chapter 54

Hi Sammy,

Thank you for your letter. I appreciate that you took the time to write it.

While I appreciate it, I don't feel any better reading it. It feels like we wasted so much time trying to figure each other out. I should've broken up with you last year when I graduated. Remember when we took pictures after the ceremony? I seriously considered it, then, calling you and ending it, ending us. Why? Because a new chapter should be just that—new. But I decided I didn't want to be without you, without my love. Now I see I was mistaken. So, better late than never, I guess. I hope you find what you're looking for.

Ryan

Chapter 55

That was mean. It came out of nowhere. Like, from the deepest, darkest depths of a heartless soul. Who even knows where that exists?

We've talked about breaking up before, definitely. But on his graduation day? That's a slap in the face, the kind that leaves an outline of a handprint for hours, but the pain continues for a while longer, until it can't do anything but disappear.

That's how I'm feeling right now. Like I've been slapped. The bitchiest of bitch slaps. And apparently, I'm the bitch.

How did we get here? To this place? The one where we can't even send mature messages to each other and end our romance cordially? I never wanted this, this ending. The mean kind. The kind where attacks are fair game and resentment reigns supreme. Where secrets are liabilities. I've had secrets, too; I know that. The difference is I never used them to hurt him. What else is he hiding? I wonder . . . .

I know his parents never liked me. They thought I made him cry all the time. Which may be true. But it doesn't make me a bad person. It just makes him human.

He's been saying all year that he thinks he's disappointing me. But really, I think he's disappointing himself. Projection at its finest. Why is he disappointed? Maybe he thinks he should've broken up with me a long time ago. And he's disappointed that he stayed in it for as long as he did.

I'm disappointed, too. I'm disappointed we couldn't end on a high note. I'm disappointed we couldn't stay friends. I'm disappointed we weren't honest with each other.

I could have told him about Dustin. And Cameron. And Todd. And Mark. (This list is way longer than I thought it could be. I am so oblivious sometimes.) But to what end? It would have probably made him even more insecure. Just look at how he reacted with Kane! And that was *after* we broke up. And none of it meant anything. Not in any meaningful way.

But then again, do I want to be with someone who is so insecure? That's not even flattering. I want to be with someone who appreciates that other people appreciate me. That they have good taste. To realize that he's the one I chose, out of all the rest of them. It's a catch-22.

I know what's missing. It's a sense of conviction, a certitude. A belief in himself. If he doesn't believe in himself, how can he expect me to?

I'd rather be alone.

Joke's on me.

Chapter 56

I've been accepted as a staff member of the BBHS *Harpoon*. I received the email today.

I pick up my phone to call Ryan . . .

. . . Before I remember that's not allowed anymore.

Chapter 57

They say the stages of grief are denial, anger, bargaining, depression, and acceptance. I've never been one to deny my feelings, though culturally half of me might beg to differ. I wouldn't say I'm angry. Resentful, maybe. Does that count as anger?

I'm depressed by the feeling of lost control. That I can't control how Ryan feels about me. Did I ever have that power, though? No. But I felt like I did. It's funny how we live in these alternate universes we create for ourselves. Our life is what our thoughts make it, says Marcus Aurelius.

He wasn't wrong.

I accept our relationship has ended. I accept that it ended in a way I would never have planned. I accept I can't control how Ryan feels about me, but I *can* control how I feel about myself, and how I move forward.

I accept I am sad, and probably will be for a while.

I accept Ryan has feelings he never shared with me. I accept that I can't control what he did and didn't share.

I accept I wouldn't have done anything differently.

But I'm still sad. I've been crying a lot. Because I miss him. I miss our friendship. I miss his support. I miss being able to text him, just because.

I accept that I'm sad.

I accept the only way forward is through it all.

Chapter 58

Thank god for summer. And family vacations.

We're leaving for Maui tomorrow. Since Daddy isn't coming as usual, everyone gets the vacation they're hoping for. Meaning, no textbooks or morning math problems.

I'm packed for the most part. I started making my packing list weeks ago. Every article of clothing is its own line item. I maintain it's the best way to keep organized. It's not like the list is even that long. I mean, it's Hawaii. Bathing suits and cover-ups are staples. Along with flip-flops and flowy dresses. I just like to map out various combinations of outfits so I can maximize the space in my suitcase.

Go ahead, judge me.

I have some summer reading I'll bring with me for US History and French. No AP Chem on this trip. I also have Honors English. Our curriculum stipulates we will read 22 books this upcoming school year. That sounds ridiculous to me. I love a good book as much as the next bibliophile, but how does a person even enjoy the quality when they're being assessed on consuming quantity?

And of course I'll bring my journal.

I take a bike ride this afternoon. I haven't been out on the bike in a while. I've been going to the beach, i.e., to lay out and take a dip in the water every half hour or so in my ritualistic manner. I think I feel sad when I bike because it reminds me of when I'd bike to Blackie's or wherever to see Ryan after a surf. It's been weird not doing that. But I'm adjusting.

I decide to head towards the Wedge today. I've always liked Jetty View Park, where the mouth of the harbor meets the ocean. It's the safety of the harbor I like, that after a long day on the ocean, there's a moor waiting for you in a sheltered place at the end of the day.

As I pass by B Street, I notice the tower guard climbing the ladder up to his seat, presumably after yelling at some skimboarders to respect the blackball.

It's him. It's Ryan.

He doesn't see me. But I see him. For all that he is.

I wonder if he ever saw me.

Thank You!

I am so appreciative of you taking the time to read my book. This novel (and series) is very personal to me, and I hope that sentiment came through in my words.

If you enjoyed *If Love Were Salt*, and would be willing to spare just two or three minutes . . . please share your review of the book on my website:

www.bysarasalam.com

Reviews help me get the book into as many hands as possible, and support my work as an author for the long-term (my dream!).

I'm grateful for your support and look forward to sharing more of my work with you!

A Note About the Author

Sara Salam is an award-winning author, editor and poet. Published since age 11, Sara writes nonfiction, fiction, and poetry. In addition to her work as an author, Sara spent seven seasons working in professional sports: five with the Boston Red Sox (2013 World Series Champion!) and two with the LA Clippers. During this time, she primarily focused on human resources strategy, including diversity and inclusion, talent acquisition, and professional development. Sara is a proud UCLA Bruin and active in her community of Newport Beach. She enjoys writing, yoga and the beach.

© 2020 Sara Salam

🌐 www.bysarasalam.com

📷 @bysarasalam

▶ Sara Salam

Acknowledgments

If Love Were Salt is the sequel to my first novel *If Water Were Fire*. The two books make up the first half of a four-part series inspired by my own life growing up in Newport Beach, California. I never thought I'd have the opportunity, let alone the capability, to produce content that is so personal and meaningful to me.

As with all of my work, my goal is to entertain, educate and empower my readers. In this novel, I incorporate details from cultural references from my South Asian heritage, to insight on what the difference between a swell and a wave is. I find value in learning new things, and I do my best to pass my own learnings along to my readers.

As always, I'm grateful for the support of family and friends who motivate me to keep going. And for my hometown, where I made my memories and turned them into meaningful messages to share with the world. I'm thankful everyday for the opportunity to write about my youth in the place where I lived it. The poetry of it all is not lost on me.

www.ingramcontent.com/pod-product-compliance
Lightning Source LLC
Chambersburg PA
CBHW050507190726
48284CB00003B/713